DEAD MAN'S TRAIL

Raine Stockton Dog Mystery #16

Donna Ball

Blue Merle Publishing

ISBN-13: 979-8-9907305-0-2

Cover design by: Donna Ball
First Published May, 2024 by Blue Merle Publishing
www.bluemerlepublishers.com
Printed in the United States of America

The ethical hunter approaches his responsibility with sobriety and honor. He respects the balance of nature and strives to preserve it. He does not countenance waste. He kills to feed himself and his family and to ensure the survival of both. He perfects his craft so that no prey shall suffer unnecessarily. He knows his place in the forest and endeavors to maintain it. The ethical hunter is essential to the survival of the species.

—The Ethical Hunter
Elijah James Waycross
1883

CHAPTER ONE

According to the National Park Service, which admits an accurate report is impossible, thousands of Americans make their permanent homes in America's vast network of national parks and forests. The number increases during times of economic downturn when families find temporary shelter in park campgrounds for two weeks at a time before moving on to begin the process over again in another park. The problem is more prominent in the Southern states where the climate is hospitable year-round, and in rural areas, where other provisions for temporary homelessness are few and far between. This population is transient, reacting to temporary circumstances they hope to improve. But there is another category of forest-dweller: those who are there by choice, who desire no other life, who have made the deep lush woods of America's backcountry their home.

Patrick Henry Jessup belonged to the latter group. His home was a tent reinforced with moss and evergreen boughs to be completely weatherproof and virtually indistinguishable from the forest itself when viewed from a distance—or even, much of the time, up close. One time a forest ranger had passed within twenty feet of Jessup's camp while Jessup watched, as still as a log, with the arrow of a crossbow centered on the back of the ranger's neck. The ranger had never once noticed the camp was there.

Jessup was nomadic by nature, like all humans once had been. To stay in one place too long was to risk over-hunting his territory, as any smart predator knew. As a general rule, he preferred national forests to national parks. Parks were over-crowded and over-regulated—Yellowstone, for example, was a travesty and a crime against what its founders had intended—but in a national forest a man could disappear. Jessup had helped quite a few of them disappear over the years, and he had perfected the process to an art.

National parks had their uses, however, particularly this time of year, when tourism slowed down and so did patrols. Most of the campgrounds closed down, which was fine with Jessup. He was mostly interested in day hikers, particularly the young and overconfident who were convinced they were invincible, and the old and the slow, who had nothing to do with their time but to try to recapture their youth and athleticism on the trails of the nation's parks. They thought they were safe there. They couldn't have been more wrong.

He met the Ringgolds on a sunrise hike along Lost Cove Trail on the North Carolina side of the Great Smoky Mountains National Park. They were from

Minnesota, in their seventies, retired, driving their RV to Florida where they had a winter home. They were staying at a KOA just off Highway 129, taking their time and enjoying the national parks along the way. Jessup walked with them for a while, chatting them up. He could be personable, even charming, when he wanted to be. That was one of his tools.

He told them he was a trail guide, and his well-worn hiking boots and faded canvas day pack added credulity to the story. To seal the deal, he pointed out a few landmarks along the trail, some bear sign and local fauna. That wasn't a hardship, since he knew the park as well as any ranger, having hunted it, off and on, for over ten years. Mary—she insisted he call her that—told him they had no children, their only relative being an aging mother in a nursing home. That was a bonus, but not necessary. Mike let drop that he had retired from an engineering firm with a nice pension, which was necessary, and greatly appreciated, information.

Jessup left them at the junction to Ford Creek Trail, told them to be careful crossing the creek, and wished them safe travels to Florida. They waved him a cheerful goodbye. Three minutes later, Jessup stepped out from behind a clump of rhododendron and slit Mike's throat with a six-inch hunting knife. He died instantly and did not suffer.

Mary was not so lucky.

CHAPTER TWO

Sometimes when I'm in a philosophical mood I think about the eagle, and how ridiculous we must all look to him as he soars so high above the earth looking down on us with his expert vision. Here we are scurrying back and forth and never really going anywhere, acting so busy and purposeful and never actually accomplishing anything, focused on things that seem so important to us but in the grand scheme of things don't matter much at all. The eagle, on the other hand, has one job: to spot his prey—a fish, a field mouse, a lizard—scoop it up, soar back to the heights and do it all over again. And that, of course, seems like a low-level, meaningless existence to us, with all our grand plans and big ambitions. My point being, it's all a matter of perspective.

I would think about perspective a lot over the next few days, how my problems and Miles's problems started out seeming so very urgent and how, if only we had known what we were really up against, they would have seemed almost incidental. How quickly the crises of the modern world lose their significance when faced with the stark realities of life and death, and how easy it is to let those realities sneak up on you when all your attention is focused on things that don't matter. In the wild, you are either the eagle or the mouse. Once you realize that, everything changes.

As for myself, I'm neither mouse nor eagle. I'm just a small-town girl from a place called Hanover County, North Carolina, in the heart of the Smoky Mountains which virtually no one has ever heard of. I'm a dog trainer—kind of—who makes her living—more or less —with a boarding and training business which used to be pretty popular. I have a degree in wildlife biology —never used—and the distinction of being a (former) part-time consultant for the forest service, which meant I worked as hard as any full-time employee for half-pay and no benefits. I'm certified, with my golden retriever, Cisco, in wilderness search and rescue and canine team therapy, but those activities, too, had mostly fallen by the wayside of late.

Everything starts with something, and for me it all began on a cold, rainy November afternoon when Miles looked up from his phone—for the first time that day, I might add—and said, "Hey, sugar, how'd you like to have some fun?"

Fun. That was a word I hardly even recognized anymore. Case in point: I was spending Black Friday, which used to be one of my busiest days of the year, sprawled out on the sofa in front of the television completely engrossed in the struggles of a young couple from Detroit as they agonized over whether to choose the house with the beach view or the house with the inground pool. Bless their hearts. Such problems people have.

We had all somehow ended up at my house, a nineteenth-century farmhouse that was half the size of Miles's mountainside contemporary mansion half a mile away, possibly because my house was where the leftovers from my aunt Mart's Thanksgiving feast had also ended up. Miles, who is quite possibly the smartest, funniest, most thoughtful man in the world, who gets me on a level no one else has ever done before and who—of all the outrageous things— actually wants to marry me, had helped Aunt Mart prepare a banquet for twenty yesterday, so naturally she thought it was only right to send dozens of Tupperware containers filled with leftovers home with us. Miles is, of course, a gourmet cook. And did I mention rich? Lest you think being engaged to someone who's that practically perfect is a slice of paradise, let me assure you he can also be a perfect jerk. I doubt we would have gotten along so well otherwise.

So there we were, on the blackest of Black Fridays, all settled into my cluttered, dog-filled living room while gray rain pinged against the windows and a fire crackled in the fireplace. Melanie, my eleven-year-old soon-to-be stepdaughter, was playing cards at a table by the fireplace while her golden retriever, Pepper, snoozed at her feet. Mischief and Magic, my twin Australian shepherds, chewed identical bones. I was stretched out on one end of the sofa with Cisco, my four-year-old golden retriever, warming my feet while Miles made himself as comfortable as possible in the small space Cisco had allowed him at the other end of the sofa. It was a cozy scene, and if I had been in a better mood, I would have been quick to acknowledge how thankful I was. It was that time of year, after all.

But I wasn't in a particularly good mood, and the cheesy television show was the best I could do in terms of distraction. I was fairly invested in the outcome, however, and I didn't answer Miles immediately. Miles then took the opportunity to prove what a jerk he could occasionally be by snatching the remote control from the coffee table and muting the television.

"Hey," I objected. "I was watching that!"

"They pick the house with the pool," he informed me.

"Yeah," agreed Melanie. She glanced up from her card game and added, "I've seen that one like a million times."

"Well, I haven't," I replied, disgruntled. "And that's stupid, anyway. The house on the beach is a whole lot nicer." At Miles's patient, meaningful look, I relented and said with a notable lack of enthusiasm, "What kind of fun?"

I'm not usually such a grouch, or at least I try not to be. But the truth is, things had not been going all that well for me since the spring, when I was arrested for murdering my brother—or half-brother, to be exact. For some reason, people are reluctant to trust their dogs to a jailbird, and since I make my living through my dog boarding and training business, that's a problem. Bad news travels through the dog community almost as fast as it does through a small town like Hansonville, and the activities that used to be my greatest source of joy—agility with my Aussies and tracking with Cisco—weren't nearly as much fun when every conversation abruptly stopped the minute I walked up, and I could feel the side glances every time I passed by.

The fact that the purported homicide victim, Casey, was at this moment sitting in front of my fireplace playing poker with Melanie didn't seem to make much of a difference to people who couldn't get that glaring headline from the *Hansonville Herald* out of their minds: *Raine Stockton Arrested in Gruesome Homicide Case.* My phone hadn't rung once requesting a therapy dog visit at the nursing home or a program on responsible pet ownership at the elementary school. I guess another place jailbirds aren't welcome is schools. No one wanted to see Cisco do his tricks at the Halloween carnival or give a tracking demonstration at the Founder's Day festival. So far, I had not been asked to step down from my volunteer positions with the humane society or breed rescue, but I figured it was only a matter of time. And the fact is, I hadn't been to a meeting of either organization since the whole thing happened. It had gotten to the point where I didn't even want to go to the grocery store anymore. Too many stares.

So, yeah. Fun? I could use a little of that. I just had my doubts about whether Miles, as amazing as he was, could provide it. And then he surprised me.

"A wilderness retreat," he said, "with survival exercises. Featuring five days and six nights of rugged outdoor life in the beautiful mountains of Tennessee."

I stared at him. "What?"

Don't get me wrong. Miles is no couch potato. I've been climbing and camping with him, and he has no trouble keeping up with me on backcountry hikes. It's just that his preferences in outdoor sports lean more toward scuba diving in Cabo or paragliding in Aruba, with the occasional Austrian ski slope thrown in for variety. Almost all of his adventures end in a swanky condo with a killer view and a hot tub. A wilderness retreat did not sound like something that would interest him at all, and I couldn't imagine how he had even found out about it.

Miles said, "You can take Cisco, and it pays a thousand dollars a day."

Cisco lifted his beautiful golden retriever head at the sound of his name, ears pricked and alert. He hadn't had much fun these last few months, either.

Casey, across the room, looked up from his cards. "Whoa, sis, if you don't take it, I will."

Casey liked to complain about financial hardship, but the truth is he was doing just fine on a government settlement for services rendered and injuries sustained. He was a talented carpenter and builder who had spent most of the summer fixing up the house he now lived in. The work was mostly completed now and construction grinds to a halt here in the mountains this time of year, so I think he was just bored. Compared to the life he'd lived for the past twenty of his twenty-nine years, I can certainly understand that.

Melanie tapped her fingernail on the table twice like the card sharp she was pretending to be and commanded shortly, "Two off the top." Casey dealt her two cards.

I sat up straight, frowning at Miles in confusion. "What are you talking about?"

Miles explained, "It's a training camp for some of the top executives in my company. The wilderness guide had to bail at the last minute, and since you're qualified and available I thought you might like the gig."

I had met some of the executives who worked for Miles. The women wore five-inch Jimmy Choos and pencil skirts, and the men wore suits so exquisitely tailored that even I—whose knowledge of men's fashion was limited to the L.L. Bean catalog—could tell they were bespoke. And Italian. I tried to picture those walking stereotypes trapped in the woods for five days. The mind boggled.

"Of course, you'll only technically be working one day," Miles added, "so the rest of the time is yours to do with as you will. I thought you might like to participate in some of the exercises. They're being taught by a fellow named Rick Steele. Yeah, that's his real name, believe it or not, and he's a real hotshot at this kind of thing."

It was only at this point that I started to believe he was serious. "I'm not a wilderness guide," I pointed out. "And I don't know anything about the mountains of Tennessee."

"Can you take a bunch of rookies out in the woods and teach them to find their way back?"

Actually, that *did* sound like fun. "Probably," I admitted cautiously. "But what makes you think I'm looking for a job? Especially working for you."

"You wouldn't be working for me," Miles replied. "You'd be working for this guy Steele. And good, honest work is the best cure I know for depression."

I bristled. "I am not depressed."

"Well, I am," Casey said, "and I'll for damn sure take a bunch of city folks on a hike in the woods for a thousand dollars a day. Seriously, Raine, get over yourself. Don't you know a gift horse when you see it?"

Casey and I had not grown up together. In fact, we'd known each other for less than a year, and he seemed determined to make up for all that lost pesky little-brother time by razzing me at every possible opportunity. To be fair, I probably did the same thing to him. We had a lot to make up for.

But before I could think of a suitably pithy reply, Melanie spoke up, disgruntled. "I don't know what you have to be depressed about," she told Casey. "You've won the last three games."

"Four," corrected Casey, placing his cards on the table. "Read 'em and weep, kid. Aces and eights. Also known as the dead man's hand."

Melanie tossed down her cards, eyes blazing, and looked to be on the verge of a temper tantrum until she realized her father was watching. He has a thing about sportsmanship. So instead of throwing something, she scowled at Casey fiercely and said, "All I've got is a pair of twos. How'd you know?"

"You got no poker face, kid," Casey replied, raking in the pile of foil-covered chocolates in the center of the table. "And you never draw on the second round if you've got a good hand. Better to cut your losses and fold."

Miles looked at Casey sternly. "Wait. You're playing poker with my eleven-year-old daughter?"

Forgetting her pique at being bested, Melanie protested, "Come on, Dad, we're just playing for chocolates."

Casey and Miles have what you might call a tenuous relationship. Given my brother's somewhat sketchy past, you can't really blame Miles for being a little protective, and Casey hasn't entirely figured out where he stands with Miles yet. The thing is, underneath it all I think they really like each other, and I usually let them work these things out for themselves. But we had been in the middle of something, and I wanted to get back to it.

I pointed out impatiently to Miles, "You're the one who taught her to play."

"Yeah, but I didn't teach her to lose." He stood and moved toward the table. "Deal me in, Casey. How about you, Raine?"

Cisco, who thinks any human movement means something good is about to happen for him, bounded off the sofa the minute Miles stood up and raced expectantly across the room. I hesitated. I'm actually not very good at poker and don't like to play—especially with Miles, who is good at everything—but Cisco wasn't the only one who was looking at me expectantly. I shrugged and agreed, "Maybe one hand."

Melanie said, "So what's a dead man's hand, anyway?"

I knew she wouldn't stay miffed at my brother for long. In the first place, with his collar-length curly blond hair and mischievous blue eyes, he has exactly the kind of playful good looks that preteen girls can't help crushing on. In the second place, I don't think he's ever met a female he couldn't charm, and that includes me.

"Two aces, two eights," Casey replied, shuffling the cards. "Spades and clubs."

"I know *that*." Melanie rolled her eyes. "What does it mean?"

Miles brought two extra chairs to the table. "Legend has it that's the hand Wild Bill Hickok was holding when he was shot to death in a saloon."

Melanie wrinkled up her nose in distaste. "Who's he?"

"A famous gunslinger and gambler in the Wild West," Miles said. "A lot of people think getting a dead man's hand is bad luck."

Casey grinned. "Unless you win with it."

"Which is rare," Miles said.

"And why I call it lucky," said Casey, dealing out the cards.

"Fold on aces and eights in stud poker," advised Miles to Melanie. "Hold in draw. What's the buy-in?"

"Five chocolates each, lady and gentleman," replied Casey. "Five card draw, nothing wild."

I brought another bag of chocolates from the kitchen, paused to toss a treat to each of the dogs— non-chocolate, of course—and took my place at the table. "So," I said to Miles, "what do you want to make a bunch of executive-types go camping in the woods in the middle of November for?"

"Insurance," he replied, picking up his cards. "All of these people may have occasion to end up in some pretty remote locations, and they're all covered by key-man insurance. We get lower rates if they receive professional survival training." He opened the betting with three chocolates from his pile of ten, which I thought was a little rich. But Miles didn't know about starting small.

We went around the table, matching Miles's bet, and I said, "So all you have to do is prove they can camp out in the woods for a week, and you get a break on your insurance? Sweet deal."

"There's a little more to it than that." He glanced at Casey. "Two."

Casey dealt Miles two more cards and Miles added to me, "And it's not entirely in the woods. There's a lodge with dormitories and hot meals."

"Naturally." I rolled my eyes, Melanie-style. "And a wine cellar and a French chef, no doubt."

"Sounds like my kind of place," Casey said. He prompted me, "Stand or draw?"

I glanced at my cards. "I'll take two, I guess."

"Two off the top for the pretty lady," said Casey, spinning the cards to me. Melanie giggled.

"No wine cellar," Miles said, studying his cards. "And, of course, you have to hike five miles to get there."

I looked at him with raised eyebrows. This was starting to sound a little more interesting.

Casey said to Melanie, "Whatcha gonna do, kiddo?"

"I'll take one," replied Melanie smugly, clearly indicating her superior hand. Casey was right: she had absolutely no poker face, which was not necessarily a bad thing in an eleven-year-old.

"And the dealer stands pat," Casey said, holding his cards.

Miles looked at him assessingly. "Now, you see, Mel," he said, "that could mean Casey dealt himself a pretty good hand, or..." He pushed three more chocolates into the center pile. "It could mean he's bluffing."

Casey smiled and matched his bet. "We shall see."

I said, "So tell me more about this lodge in the middle of nowhere that you have to hike five miles to get to."

"That's all I know," Miles said. "I'll tell you more when I get back."

I was surprised. "You're going?"

"I'm the keynote speaker," he informed me.

Melanie said, "Hey, cool! Can I go?"

"Sorry, sweetie," Miles said. "Employees and instructors only. You're staying with Grandma." She started to pout until he added, "And don't you have a project due next week?"

Her expression brightened. "We're doing a presentation on Mesopotamian culture and I'm the team leader," she told Casey. "We're baking flatbread on a rock."

"Save me a piece," Casey replied.

She grinned. "Okay. With honey."

I frowned. "Since when do wilderness retreats have keynote speakers? And you never go to these kinds of things."

"This one is different. Like I said, it sounds like fun."

"You didn't say anything about being out of town next week."

"That's because I just decided to go. So what are you going to do, sugar?"

I should have known right then that something was off. Generally, I'm a lot better at sizing up a situation than that. But at that moment Cisco, who had been sniffing around for crumbs from his one meager treat, came over and plopped down at my feet with a great sigh, laying his head on his paws. I felt a familiar tug at my heartstrings.

I am of the firm belief that when you bring a dog into your life you take on full responsibility—for his health, safety, happiness, and mental well-being. I had made a commitment to all my dogs to give them every opportunity to reach their full potential, and it shamed me to admit I hadn't been doing a very good job of that lately.

I made a perfunctory effort to take the Aussies through their agility paces each day, mostly because they needed some way to burn off the excess energy. But they knew when they weren't competing and it showed, just like Cisco knew that a walk in the woods wasn't the same as a life-or-death search for a missing victim. I tried to keep in shape with daily hikes and seek-and-find exercises, but we hadn't been to a tracking class since early summer. I had taken my name off the search-and-rescue call list during that whole business with Casey and the trial, and I hadn't gotten around to putting it back on. Every dog needs a job, just like every human needs a purpose. I had let Cisco down, big time.

Cisco looked up at me from the floor with a baleful expression that only a golden retriever with his head on his paws can perfect. I gave a single decisive nod of my head and said, "Okay, count me in. I'll go."

It was only when everyone looked at me that I realized Miles had been talking about poker. I parted with three more of my chocolates and added quickly, "And I'll call."

Miles said, "We leave first thing in the morning. It's a two-hour drive to the trailhead and about an hour's hike. Steele will want to go through orientation with you before the rest of the people get there."

"Tomorrow?" I stared at him. "That's kind of short notice, isn't it? Corny doesn't even get back from vacation until Sunday night, and I don't have anybody to stay with Mischief and Magic."

Corny was my head groomer and general manager

of the boarding kennel. He lived on-site and was my go-to dog sitter whenever I had to be away. With business so slow, he had taken the opportunity to spend Thanksgiving with his cousins in Pennsylvania, and I certainly had no reason to object. Who knew I'd receive a last-minute invitation to take Cisco on a wilderness expedition?

"Do you have an equipment list?" I went on, my mind racing ahead. "If we need anything, we'll have to go to Asheville this afternoon, and in this weather, it'll take forever. I don't like to leave the dogs with no one in the house, but maybe your mother could look in on them…"

"Relax," Casey said, "I'll stay with the dogs. It's what? One night? Not like I've got somewhere I need to be."

That was, of course, exactly what I was hoping he would say. But before I could thank him, he said, "All right, ladies and gent, let's see what you've got."

Melanie, grinning, put down a pair of sevens and a pair of eights. "Not bad, huh?"

"Beats me to a pulp," Casey said and showed nothing but two sixes. "Always listen to your dad, Miss Mel. I was bluffing."

Miles put down two fives. "Looks like it's your game so far, Mel. What've you got, Raine?"

"Two eights." I put down my cards without looking at them. "It usually takes a couple of days to pack for something like this, you know. It's not just my stuff, it's…"

"Hey, look at that!" Melanie exclaimed. Everyone

was staring at my cards.

"What?" I said.

Melanie pointed to my cards. "Guess this means you're lucky, Raine."

"What are the odds?" Casey murmured.

"Yeah," agreed Miles, looking at him suspiciously. "What are the odds?"

Casey spread his hands in protest. "Come on, man. I wouldn't even know how."

"Yeah, but I still win, right?" Melanie insisted.

"Sorry, sweetheart," said Miles.

Melanie folded her arms across her chest and glared at me. I looked down at the hand I had spread on the table, noticing it for the first time. Ace of spades, ace of clubs, eight of clubs, eight of spades, and a queen. Dead man's hand.

"Huh," I said. I glanced uncertainly at Miles. "How'd that happen?"

"Pure luck," Casey told me with a grin. "Just like I said."

"Maybe." Miles started gathering up the cards. "But just in case your luck doesn't hold, I'll deal the next round."

I started to point out that the hand couldn't be all that lucky if a dead man had been holding it, but that seemed like tempting fate.

And as it turns out, it was.

CHAPTER THREE

I'd kept an emergency backpack stocked for both myself and Cisco for the past fifteen years, so despite what I'd told Miles, it took about ten minutes for me to glance over the list he'd given me and supplement my supplies. Cisco would carry a week's worth of dehydrated dog food and treats in his saddlebags, collapsable food and water bowls, a tightly folded chamois that would serve as both a towel for quick dry-offs and a lightweight sleeping mat, a canine first aid kit, rubber booties in case we ran into rough terrain, and a couple of Nylabones and a chew toy for down time. My pack was a little more complicated, but going through it, checking and repacking every essential, gave me that same sense of relaxed confidence that a concert pianist might feel as his fingers glided over the keys—easy, comforting, familiar. I was in my element again.

Casey arrived at 7:00 a.m., thirty minutes after I'd asked him to be there. My brother is many things, but punctual is not one of them. Miles had already loaded the SUV and was leaning against the car door, sipping his coffee and pretending not to be impatient. Cisco, who knew an adventure was in store the minute he saw me take out his backpack, pranced around the kitchen with a stuffed squirrel in his mouth, hardly able to contain his excitement and wondering what the holdup was.

I opened the door to admit Casey and a draft of cold, damp air, scolding, "For heaven's sake, Casey, we were supposed to leave half an hour ago!"

The three dogs rushed him and Casey, knowing his priorities, dropped to his knees to greet them with enthusiastic ear rubs and pats. Casey is good with dogs—a genetic trait, no doubt—and the dogs love him, otherwise, I would have never left him in charge of Mischief and Magic until Corny returned.

"Sorry," he told me when his most important duty was done. "I overslept. Do you know it's pitch-dark at six o'clock in the morning around here?"

"I do know that," I informed him tartly. "Do you know how I know? Because that's what time I was up waiting for you to get here."

Casey just grinned and got to his feet, albeit a little stiffly. "Well, I'm here now. Have a good time. I wish I was going with you."

I had no doubt that was what he wished, but we both knew Casey's days of outdoor adventuring were over, at least for a while. He was still recovering from an accident that had almost taken his life and left him with three metal rods in his leg—and that was just for starters. He wouldn't have made it halfway through the hike to the lodge.

Now I was sorry I'd been short with him, and I said, not entirely insincerely, "Maybe next time. Anyway," I went on hurriedly, "the girls have had their breakfast. They get a snack in the afternoon but don't overload them with treats. Here's the dog food…" I opened the cabinet to show him. "And the feeding instructions are taped on the inside of the door, here."

"I've seen you feed them like a hundred times," he reminded me.

"Don't let them outside unless you're with them," I went on. "They can climb the fence in a flash if they get bored. You can throw the ball for them or play Frisbee if they get too rambunctious, but mostly you just have to hang out and watch football until Corny gets back. There are plenty of leftovers in the fridge and a whole platter of Aunt Mart's cookies. If you have any problems…"

"I won't," he assured me.

I filled my travel mug with coffee. "I don't think we have cell service in this place, so don't worry if you don't hear from me. You can always call Melanie if you have any questions about the dogs. She knows where everything is. She'll probably be down here pestering you to death all day anyway."

He said, "I got this, sis."

I turned, smiling at him apologetically as I twisted the lid back onto my coffee mug. "I know you do."

I gave Mischief and Magic a quick hug and took Cisco's hiking leash down from its hook. At this, Cisco spun around in double circles, barely able to contain his excitement. That made us both laugh.

"Well," I said, glancing around the kitchen for anything I might have forgotten. "I guess that's it. I'll see you Friday."

"Hold on a minute," Casey said. "I got you something." He reached into the pocket of his denim jacket and took out a slender box, offering it to me. "I was going to save it for Christmas, but I figured you could use it now."

"Casey..." I took the box uncertainly and opened it. My eyes widened. It was a digital watch. "Oh, wow." This was hardly a casual gift, certainly not the kind of thing an unemployed carpenter would buy on impulse, not even for Christmas. "Casey, you shouldn't..." But then I stopped and looked at him suspiciously. "Wait. You *did* buy this, didn't you?"

He returned a dry look. "Relax. My days of dealing hot merchandise are over. Or," he admitted, "at least as far as I know. I got it in a pawn shop in Asheville. Good deal, too." He took it out of the box to show me. "It's a hiker's watch," he explained. "It's got a built-in compass and GPS locator, all hooked up to a satellite in case you lose cell service. Twenty-four-hour weather forecast, too. And look. You push this button on the side three times, and it sends a message to your emergency contact. In case you fall off a cliff or, I don't know, get mauled by a bear or something. I programmed in my number for now, but you'll probably want to change it to Miles's when you get back."

I ignored the remark about being mauled by a bear

and admired the watch as I strapped it on my wrist. "Cool," I said, impressed. I smiled up at him. "Thanks, Casey. I mean it. This is really something."

"There's a seven-day charge on it," he said, "so you should be okay 'til you get back. The charger and the instructions are in the box."

I hugged him. "You're the best."

When we stepped apart his expression was serious. "Raine," he said, "I just wanted to tell you... I feel bad, you know, about everything that's happened. I know your life was a lot better before I showed up and..."

I interrupted him with a fierce shake of my head. "Don't say that. That's not true."

"Sure it is," he replied, not arguing, just stating the facts. "You used to have a good business, lots of friends. You were always doing cool things and going fun places. I was jealous of you, remember? Now..."

"Not so much," I supplied for him. I tried, and failed, to smile.

"Anyway," he said, "I just wanted to say I'm sorry."

I didn't know what to say. There were a lot of things I should have said, and I would think of them all later because hindsight is twenty-twenty. But at that moment all I could mutter was something stupid like, "It's not your fault."

I hugged him quickly again and added, "We need to get on the road. Thanks again. You know, for the watch and..." I hoped my smile looked more genuine than it felt. "Everything."

"You bet."

He caught the Aussies' collars as they tried to follow Cisco out the door, and as I glanced back, he winked at me. "Don't get mauled by a bear."

I made a face and gave him a perfunctory wave goodbye, thinking what a nice picture that would have made: Casey kneeling on the floor with my two gorgeous girls on either side of him. I wish I'd taken it.

CHAPTER FOUR

There is something purely mystical about the Smoky Mountain range, something ancient and unsettling, yet at the same time profoundly familiar. The waterfalls that sluice down black granite canyon walls, the wide, white-water rivers that echo the taste of prehistoric times, the deep pine forest cathedrals…there are many uniquely beautiful places in the world, I know, but none that speak to the human soul quite like the Smoky Mountains.

It is not a friendly place. There are coves and hollows deep within the forests of the Great Smoky Mountains National Park that have never known a human footprint. The largest population of black bears in the Eastern United States live here, as do dozens of far more aggressive species of animal, reptile, and insect. It has been said that everything a human being needs to survive can be found in these mountains. But also in these mountains are at least as many things waiting to kill you.

It goes without saying that anyone entering this wilderness unprepared does so at his peril. We are guests here, far outside our natural habitat, and those who approach the mysteries of these dark mountains as though they were spending a weekend at summer camp are very often never seen again. I should know. I've spent more hours than I can count searching for them.

I have led wilderness expeditions like this before, but generally on my own turf. I know every trail, abandoned logging road, gorge, cliff, and deer path in Hanover County and most of the surrounding area. I grew up swinging from the trees and sliding down the waterfalls there. But I am not foolish enough to think even for one minute that one piece of mountain wilderness is just like another.

I had therefore fallen asleep the previous night studying the trail maps of the area surrounding our base camp—appropriately called Hidden Lodge—and I spent the first part of our drive reviewing the maps on my phone. The lodge, with its thirty-two-acre property, abutted national park land and was surrounded by some fairly inhospitable terrain. The nearest ranger station was twenty-eight miles away via paved roads and virtually inaccessible across country. The nearby trails, with names like Dead Man's Trail, Broken Arrow Pass, and Forgotten Trace, were not marked as being maintained by the park service. They were not day hikes.

"Say, listen to this," I said, thumbing the screen. "Two bodies were found in the woods abutting Dead

Man's Trail, about four miles from the lodge, 2000 and 2005. Never identified."

"Huh," said Miles, eyes on the twisty road. "Guess that's how it got its name."

"I guess. Not that unusual, though." I glanced at him. "People go missing in the woods all the time. It's just a shame they were never identified."

Miles said, "Better download those maps, sugar. My understanding is that we lose cell phone service about a hundred feet from the parking lot."

I looked up to discover we were well into Great Smoky Mountains National Park territory and about to cross the Oconaluftee River. I craned my neck to get a view of the wide, slow-moving waterway below, and Cisco, sensing something of interest might be forthcoming, sat up in the backseat and fogged up Miles's window with his hot breath as he tried to see what had caught my attention. A few kayakers had braved the early-morning cold, but otherwise, the river was as pristine as the day it had been created.

I turned back to Miles. "We're not really taking a bunch of rookies into the wilderness with no way to communicate with the outside world, are we?" I had had this argument once before, when I was hired to take a group of so-called juvenile delinquents on a three-day trek up a mountain. It turned out the people in charge were more delinquent than the juveniles were, and I had won that argument. Emergency communications are one of the most important survival tools in anybody's toolbelt.

Miles said, "Steele has a sat phone and a radio in

case of emergency. But this really is roughing it, babe."

I downloaded the maps. "So tell me about this Steele guy."

"I've never met him," Miles admitted. "He was recommended by the head of my security department and approved by the insurance carrier. Former Navy Seal and survival trainer for the military. Now he mostly does these training camps for private corporations and coordinates hostage rescue in high-risk areas around the world."

"Wow," I said. "This guy sounds serious." What I meant was that a trainer of his caliber sounded like overkill for a bunch of Ivy League suits trying to learn how to build a campfire, but I managed to put it more tactfully. "I still don't understand why you—I mean, your insurance company—think your executives need to learn how to survive in the Smoky Mountain wilderness. I thought you mostly built hotels and condos and stuff."

Of course, I did know that Miles's business was far more diversified than that, and that his interests reached all over the world, but have made it a point not to dig too deeply into the details. Fewer headaches that way.

He smiled at the simplification. "In the first place," he said, "it's not just the Smokies. In fact, this camp was supposed to be held in Canada, but there was some kind of foul-up with the paperwork. We have another camp in New Mexico that puts the students in desert terrain, and my people will have to certify in both courses to qualify for overseas placement. In the second place, we also build bridges and hospitals and factories, sometimes in places where the only value a life has is what it can be ransomed for. But I don't doubt some of my people are asking the same question. That's one of the reasons I wanted to be here."

"One of the reasons?" I prompted.

He hesitated a moment longer than it should have taken to answer a simple question. Miles doesn't lie—not to me, at least—but he has a way of being very creative with his answers. He said, "I wanted to spend some time with you, of course."

I studied his profile. It revealed very little, as usual. "And?"

"I don't get a chance to spend much face time with these people. This seemed like a good opportunity to see how they perform under stress."

That was reasonable. But there was more. I pushed. "And?"

A slight divot formed between his brows, and he seemed to debate whether to answer. Then he said carefully, "There's been some trouble at work. Someone may be passing on proprietary information to our competitors. These people, the ones who are coming to this retreat, are working on a top-secret project. I want to make sure none of them are involved."

"Wow," I said. I put away my phone, staring at him. "Way to bury the lede."

The faintest of smiles tugged at his lips. "I did promise you adventure."

"Fun," I corrected. "You promised me fun."

The smile faded, and I could tell he was more troubled than his words indicated. "It's not a big deal, Raine. Most of these people I've known for years. A couple are new on board, but if I didn't trust them, I wouldn't have hired them. It's just a matter of being double-sure."

"Insurance," I prompted.

"Right."

I come from a law-enforcement family. My uncle Ro, the former sheriff of Hanover County, says I would make a good cop, but I don't have the patience for it. What I do have, however, is a tracking dog's instinct for sensing when something is off and getting to the bottom of it.

I said, "Didn't you say this retreat had been scheduled for months?"

"Since August."

"And the people who are coming, they signed up back then?"

"Everyone except you, me, and Cisco."

"So what happened yesterday that made you drop everything and decide to come?"

He took his time forming an answer. "There was another security breach. Only this one was a trap, specifically designed to entice someone who was involved with the Salus project."

"That would be the top-secret project that all these people are working on."

"Right. But it doesn't necessarily prove anything. Like I said, not a big deal. Yet."

"Just enough for you to spend all day yesterday on your phone and make a last-minute decision to drop everything and go wilderness hiking for a week," I clarified. "So what am I doing here? Wait, let me guess. I'm your cover. Because if the boss suddenly shows up unannounced at a thing like this everyone would be suspicious. But if he brought his girlfriend..."

"Fiancée," Miles corrected, "who also happens to be a wilderness expert with a tracking dog, perfectly qualified for the job."

"Damn it, Miles." I flung myself back against the seat, arms folded across my chest, fuming. It was a moment before I could even speak. "Is there even a job?" I demanded. "Or am I supposed to just hang around looking stupid all week?"

"The job is legitimate," he replied, scowling, "and you couldn't look stupid if you tried. I should have told you the whole story..."

"You think?" I interrupted sharply.

"But I didn't *know* the whole story," he continued, the scowl deepening. "I still don't. So maybe we could just calm down and see how things play out, okay? In the meantime, there's no reason for you to worry about any of this. Just enjoy the retreat."

I muttered, "So far it sounds like a blast."

If I were completely honest with myself, I wasn't all that surprised that Miles had an ulterior motive for this trip. His life might seem as complicated as an air-traffic control pattern at an international airport, but I knew it was all very rational and strategically planned—from his point of view, anyway. He kept it that way by managing details and avoiding impulsive decisions. I should have known that anything that took him into an internet-and-phone-free zone—and away from his daughter—for an extended period had to be important. But I also knew that trying to pry answers out of him when he didn't want to give them was a waste of energy.

So I did what I always do. I took matters into my own hands. I opened up my internet browser and spent the rest of the trip getting answers.

CHAPTER FIVE

Jessup disposed of Mike's body in several different places throughout the Cherokee National Forest, covering the remains with dead leaves to assist in decomposition and make them easier for carnivores to access. It was the most efficient and ecologically sound method of disposing of a carcass, human or animal. The earth itself was a hungry hunter.

He spent several days driving the RV around to various ATMs, availing himself of the cash in the Ringgold's checking account and credit cards via the PIN Mary had eventually supplied him. By this time Mary had unfortunately expired from her injuries, but CCTV tapes and bank records would show that both Ringgolds had been alive and using their bank cards days after their deaths and a hundred miles from the KOA where they had last registered. Jessup used Mike's credit card to pay two weeks in advance for an RV site at another KOA, this one in Tennessee, and bought a twenty-five-year-old pickup truck from an ad in the paper. He then prepared to dispose of Mary's body in the same manner he had her husband's.

Jessup considered himself an ethical hunter. He took only what he needed. He wasted nothing. He left no trace of his presence and shared his kills with the carrion-eaters of the forest. He was patient, he was cautious, he was wise. In this way, he had been allowed to live his life free from molestation for over sixty years.

One of the most essential factors in escaping detection was to avoid patterns. Choosing victims of a single ilk for example—only females, only blondes, only elderly, only single—was the most common mistake and would almost always lead to discovery. The outside world loved patterns like that because they were so easy to spot. Another common mistake was taking too often from a single location. Jessup was intimately familiar with parks, forests, and wild lands from Montana to Florida and all points in between. His livelihood, after all, depended upon it. Finally, it was essential to avoid a single dumping ground or disposing of the remains too close to the kill site. To do so was to invite detection and, therefore, the end of one's career.

That was why Jessup took the time and the trouble to drive his new truck, with Mary's remains packed in a cooler in the back, to a remote area on the eastern edge of the Great Smoky Mountains National Park, where he would hike several miles into the wilderness to complete the disposal. Like all creatures of the wild, he could smell winter coming, and his time in this part of the country was almost done. Soon he would

be heading south.
    But first, one last thing.

CHAPTER SIX

We arrived at the trailhead an hour and a half later. If it hadn't been for the fancy nav system in Miles's car that used geographic coordinates instead of destination tags, I don't know that we ever would have found it. The parking lot amounted to a shallow dirt pull-off beside a winding, one-lane road bordered by a steep gully on one side and a rhododendron thicket on the other. There was a painted wooden sign that read "Hidden Lodge," and we parked beside it. The arrow beneath the writing pointed to a narrow, leaf-covered trail that was barely discernable between the undergrowth.

Miles and I got out of the SUV and surveyed our surroundings silently. I looked around uneasily. "Do you think it's safe to leave your car here?"

He replied, "Who could ever find it?"

He had a point. I summoned enthusiasm, "Well. You promised adventure."

He looked more dubious. "Did I?"

I took a selfie of the three of us and sent it to

Casey with the caption, "Starting out." In a moment he texted back a picture of Mischief and Magic stretched out on my sofa and the caption, "Staying in." That made me smile.

I showed the picture to Miles, and he remarked, "A perfect argument for why dogs are smarter than people."

I grinned and elbowed him good-naturedly. I had gotten over being mad at him about ten miles back. "Come on, sport. Let's hike."

Miles got our packs out of the back of the car while I fitted Cisco with his saddlebags and clipped his hiking leash to my belt. Five minutes later we were strapped into our backpacks and pushing through the overhanging branches and tangled vines that marked the trail. This time of year, the leaves covering the ground were so thick that even calling it a trail was pure speculation. Clearly, no one had been this way in a while.

We traveled single file with Miles—who was very good about bending back sapling limbs and thorny branches so they didn't slap me in the face—taking point. I checked my phone a few hundred yards in and, sure enough, zero bars.

I said, "You're sure they're expecting us, right? This trail looks pretty abandoned."

Miles, ducking under a low-hanging rope of smoke vine, replied, "Part of the charm, sweetheart."

After about twenty minutes the trail cleared out and started to look more like a path than a suggestion. It was still slow going, though, as we stopped to move fallen saplings out of the way and skirted rocks the size of Volkswagens, doing our best to sweep away the heavy cover of dead leaves with our feet so that those who came behind us would at least have a hint as to where the trail lay. Cisco was having the time of his life, but I was breathing hard after a mile. "Okay," I said, "do people seriously *pay* to stay here?"

"Not often, from the looks of it," he agreed. He gestured toward a fading slash of white paint on a tree up ahead. "At least we know we're headed in the right direction."

I stopped and braced my hands on my knees for a minute, catching my breath. "So how did you hear about this place, anyway?"

"I didn't." Miles took out his water bottle and unscrewed the top. "Steele picked the location. Apparently, it was built as a hunting lodge in the 1920s. They used horses to get up there then. The park service took over the operation of the lodge in the 1960s, although the surrounding acreage, thirty or so I think, is still considered private land. That's why we're able to use it for things not usually allowed inside state parks, like open fires and dogs. There've been a few renovations to the lodge..."

"Indoor plumbing?" I suggested.

He grinned and took a drink from his water bottle. "Afraid not. Not even hot water, as far as my research revealed."

I shrugged and adjusted my expectations. I actually liked roughing it, although cold showers in the middle of the winter were not anybody's idea of fun.

I poured water into Cisco's collapsible bowl and drank from my own bottle while he lapped it up. "What about food?"

"There's a generator," he said, "and a site manager who stocks the pantry."

I grinned at him and took another sip of my water. "I knew it. French chef, wine cellar."

He grinned back. "You read the rules. No alcohol, no firearms. Also"—he recapped his bottle and put it away—"no French chef. I think we're talking chili-mac and tuna casserole, here."

"Better than MREs," I pointed out. Although, truth be told, I didn't think the freeze-dried camp food was half as bad as people made out.

We pushed on, and I could feel the trail start to steepen in the burning in the back of my legs. Miles told me that the five executives who would be participating in the retreat were approximately three hours behind us and would be dropped off at the trailhead via shuttle. I thought that was as good a time as any to reopen the subject of why we were really here.

"Parker Sandoval," I said, "age forty-three, head of overseas operations, employed nine. Barbara Valentine, also known as BJ, age thirty-nine, corporate counsel for the past six years. Maxine Hodges, age 54, finance and accounting, three years. Reed Barnes..."

He shot me an annoyed look. "What did you do, hack my e-mail?"

"No," I replied mildly, "I went on the park service

web site, sent a text to the lodge manager for a list of the guests, and let Google do the rest."

"Sounds like something Casey would do. Or Melanie."

Now *I* was annoyed. "I don't need either one of them to show me how to work the internet." Although the truth was, I had picked up more than a few shortcuts from Casey over the past few months, some of which might not have been entirely legal. "May I continue?"

"I'll save you the trouble," he answered. It seemed to me he lengthened his stride, but I kept up determinedly. "Reed Barnes and Theo Carter, both in R&D, are former VPs with Versatech. I brought them over when I acquired Versatech two years ago. They flew in from Italy this morning to be here."

"So which one of them do you think is a thief?"

Just to show he was over his pique with me, he paused and held up a thorny branch for me to pass under. With exaggerated patience, he explained, "None of them. Like I said, this is just a double-check."

That was BS and he knew I knew it. For the sake of harmony, I was once again forced to ty to hide my annoyance. "Could you at least tell me what, exactly, you think they've stolen?"

"I could," he replied equitably, letting the branch fall back into place once Cisco and I were through. "But then I'd have to kill you."

He smiled sweetly at me, but I returned only a sour look. "So do they even know you're going to be there?"

"Group text this morning," he assured me. "They'll

be thrilled. I'm beloved, you know."

That almost made me laugh. I once again tried, and failed, to imagine a bunch of soft-muscled corporate types following in our footsteps. One thing was certain: They would not be in a very good mood when they eventually arrived at the lodge. If, in fact, they did. And those guys who were getting off a plane from sunny Italy to go hiking in the wilderness in forty-degree weather? They were going to be nothing less than pissed.

We came to a half-rotten log that had fallen across the path, and Miles bent to grasp one end. "Give me a hand, honey."

I braced my legs and got my hands under the other end of the log, and we managed to swing it to the side of the trail.

"You can't tell me they haul in supplies over this trail to the lodge," I said, dusting off my hands on my pants. "What do they use, mules?"

"There's a logging road behind the lodge for staff and deliveries," Miles said, moving forward on the trail. "Completely accessible."

I stopped and stared at him until he turned around. "Do you mean to tell me," I demanded, "we could have *driven* to the lodge?"

He grinned. "I thought you wanted to have fun."

I returned what I hoped was a forbidding scowl and pushed past him to take the lead.

The truth was it was exhilarating to be back in the woods again. It was too late in the season for the trees to have retained their colorful leaves, but the view through the bare branches was still spectacular when we came upon an unexpected bend in the trail that overlooked a vista of lavender and blue mountaintops swathed in smoky clouds. Yesterday's storm was far behind us, and the sky was a crystal cobalt, the sun sparkling on our faces through the network of stripped branches. The air was crisp and just cool enough to keep us from breaking a sweat as we hiked. Cisco bounded along beside me on his bungee leash, oblivious to the weight of his saddlebags, his nose twitching and his eyes darting happily from one potential target to another. He was a tracking dog, and he was ready to get to work.

"Not yet," I told him, reaching down to ruffle his fur affectionately. "But soon."

We passed a gorgeous waterfall, after which the trail leveled off across a wide stretch of mossy glade. It really was paradise.

Paradise ended with the sound of water bubbling noisily over rocks. By this time Miles was a couple of dozen yards ahead of us, and when we caught up with him, he was standing on the bank of a wide, shallow creek. "So," he said, "I guess we're supposed to cross."

I shaded my eyes against the sun and squinted across to the opposite bank, where I could barely make out another white hash mark on a tree. "It doesn't look to be more than two or three feet deep," I said. "You'll get wet, but you won't drown."

He cast me a mildly disparaging look. "I," he informed me, "don't intend to do either."

I watched, grinning, as Miles picked his way

carefully and expertly across the smooth rocks that provided the only bridge across the waterway. When he reached the other side, he took the three-foot leap in a single bound and landed on dry land. His boots hadn't even gotten splashed.

He cupped his hands and called to me, "Take your time. It's doable. Just be careful."

Like I'd never crossed a creek before.

I unclipped Cisco's leash from my belt and wrapped it around his neck, securing it to itself so he wouldn't get tangled up. I then removed his saddlebags and balanced them over my shoulders. "Cisco first!" I called back to Miles.

Miles squatted down on the creek bank and opened his arms for Cisco. I flung my arm out toward Miles and told Cisco, "Go, Cisco! Go find Miles!"

In the first place, Cisco loved Miles and we played the "go find" game all the time at home. In the second place, he knew perfectly well Miles had dog biscuits in his pack. Cisco didn't hesitate, and he didn't bother trying to stay on the rocks. He splashed across the creek, paddling when it grew too deep, and scrambled onto the bank, spraying a laughing Miles with cold creek water as he shook off his coat. I waited until Miles unwrapped Cisco's leash and rewarded him with a dog biscuit before I started across. If you think it's easy hopping from slippery rock to slippery rock while carrying a thirty-pound pack on your back *and* eight pounds of dog supplies across your shoulders, let me assure you it is not. But I only slipped once, and even then I managed to keep my socks dry.

Miles extended his hand to help me onto the bank, and we both decided it was time for a break. We found a clearing a little farther from the water and shed our packs, and while Miles unpacked roast beef sandwiches on crispy baguettes with fresh oranges and vitamin water for us, I gave Cisco a canine protein bar and filled his collapsible bowl with water. Miles and I leaned against our packs and stretched out our legs as we ate, enjoying the warmth of the sun and the murmur of the creek. Cisco lay beside us, patchy sunlight glinting on his golden fur as he chewed a stick he'd found at the edge of the woods. His crunching was a counterpoint to the distant cry of a hawk and the chittering of squirrels.

"How much farther, do you suppose?" I glanced at my watch. "We've been on the trail for over an hour."

He opened his hand. "Let me see your watch."

I unfastened it and handed it over.

"This was nice of Casey," he said. He pushed some buttons and tapped some screens on the watch face. "I wish I'd thought of it."

"Yes," I agreed, although a little uncertainly. "It was."

He knew me well enough to know there was more, and he looked at me curiously. "But?" he prompted.

I shrugged one shoulder uncomfortably. "It's nothing. It's stupid. It's just…" I glanced at him and then away. "I think Casey is planning to leave."

Miles seemed to consider that. "Why do you think so?"

"He's bored. He's almost recovered from his surgery

now and there's no reason for him to hang around. There's nothing for him in a small town like Hansonville."

"There's you," Miles pointed out.

I dismissed that with a shake of my head. "Not enough." *Besides*, I thought but did not say, *everyone leaves me, eventually*. I knew it was self-pitying, but it was also a simple fact, and one I had come to understand all too well recently.

Miles shrugged one shoulder. "You could be right. Casey's not very reliable."

Despite the fact that I had said it first, this made me bristle. "You've never liked Casey."

"I like him fine," Miles insisted, for not the first time. "I just don't trust him. Never did, never will."

"Terrific." All the glow had gone out of the day and I glared at him, arms folded across my chest. "Could you just tell me one thing, Miles? Why did you wait until we're in the middle of nowhere and about to be stuck with each other for five days before you decide to pick a fight with me? First, you lie to me about why I'm even here..."

"I did not lie."

"Then you tell me this crazy story about some kind of corporate intrigue and won't even give me a straight answer about it when *I'm* the one who was dragged all the way out here..."

"I didn't drag you anywhere," he returned, irritated.

"And now you're picking on my brother for no good reason at all! If this is the way the week is going to go,

I wish I'd stayed at home."

"And if this is the way you're going to react to every little thing I say," Miles returned shortly, "maybe you should have."

I glowered at him for another long moment and then started stuffing the remnants of our picnic into my backpack with angry, jerky motions. Cisco, who could always sense tension between the people he loved, stopped gnawing his stick and looked worriedly from Miles to me.

Miles placed what was supposed to be a calming hand atop my arm. "Stop pouting for a minute and listen, will you? I'm about to apologize."

I jerked my arm away.

"All right," he admitted. "Maybe I was trying to start a fight. I'm sorry. But, babe, I know you…"

"Well enough to play me on Broadway, I know," I interrupted curtly, zipping up my pack. "Sorry to be so damn predictable."

"You're like that fish that has to be shipped to market in a tank with a predator because if it's not kept in a constant state of high stimulation its flesh becomes soft and inedible," he said. "If you're not living on the edge, you're not living. And, sugar, these past few months you've hardly been living at all."

I stared at him. "You're comparing me to a fish? That's your apology?"

He held out my watch with a rueful smile. "Here."

I took the watch grudgingly. Instead of the time of day, the watch face now showed a squiggly line with a blinking red dot at the bottom and latitude and longitude coordinates at the top. A message scrolled across the middle. "Distance to destination 1.35 miles." I was in no mood to give him a compliment, but I have to admit, I was impressed.

I asked reluctantly, "How'd you do that?"

"I have the same app on my smart watch," he said.

"Oh, yeah?" I strapped the watch back on my wrist. "Who does yours call in an emergency?'"

"My security team."

I looked at him skeptically. "In Atlanta?"

I had the satisfaction of seeing him momentarily disconcerted. "I guess that's a little more practical in urban areas than out here."

"I'm not sure it's practical anywhere," I said. "It just gives you a false since of security."

He shrugged. "Maybe."

Cisco, acknowledging the release of tension between us, had returned to his stick. But now he suddenly stopped gnawing and looked up, his ears pricked, his eyes focused intently on the woods behind me. A low, almost inaudible growl rumbled in his throat.

I put my hand on Miles's arm and felt his muscles stiffen with attention. He, too, was watching Cisco. "There's something out there," I whispered.

I twisted around to look, and Miles started to get to his feet. Suddenly Cisco leapt up, barking furiously at the woods. I scrambled to my feet and whirled around, but too late.

A man was already standing there, less than three feet away from me, gripping a knife in his hand.

CHAPTER SEVEN

I silenced Cisco with a quick turn of my palm and he sat down, licking his lips and shifting his weight anxiously. I crouched down and slipped my fingers under his collar, my heart pounding. It's not Cisco's job to protect me; it's my job to protect him. And the guy was holding a 9-inch blade.

He was a big-muscled man with a gray crew cut and sharp blue eyes. A scar ran from one of those eyes to his temple. He wore a day pack and all-weather camos with hiking boots. His jaw was set in grim disapproval as he looked at Cisco and slowly returned his knife to the leather scabbard on his belt. With the same motion, he tossed away the handful of vines he had apparently just cut.

Miles extended his hand. "Rick Steele, I presume."

The other man shook his hand firmly. "Mr. Young." He looked at me, eyes unreadable. "And this is your wilderness guide." There was no particular expression in his voice, nor did his face change when he looked at me. Then why did I think I sensed contempt when he spoke?

"Raine Stockton," Miles supplied.

I straightened up and started to offer my own hand, but Steele said flatly, "You brought a dog."

"I told you we were going to," Miles said.

I added, "This is Cisco, he's a certified…"

"You made a couple of mistakes," Steele interrupted. "First, you sat with your back to the wood line. Anything could have come at you before you knew it. Second…" With a surprisingly swift motion, he reached down and swept up my backpack. "You took your eyes off your pack. This pack can be the difference between life and death out here, and now you don't have it anymore, do you?"

My cheeks burned with anger and embarrassment, but it was outrage that prompted my exclamation of "Hey!" when he unzipped my backpack and started going through the contents. I took a step forward to snatch the pack from him and Cisco came with me, eager to make the acquaintance of the stranger. The stranger, however, stopped us both with a glare.

"You're on my team," he said, "I inspect your pack."

I had no reasonable objection to that, so I just muttered, "Don't mess up my stuff."

Cisco continued to creep forward, step by step, grinning his silly golden retriever grin as he anticipated making a new friend. I hated it, but I had to jerk him back sharply. Already I could tell this man did not want to be our friend.

Cisco sat at my side with a reproachful look, which did nothing for my temperament. I said irritably to

Steele, "And just so we're clear, we didn't *have* to watch the wood line. Cisco was watching it for us."

"And he'd still be barking after I'd cut your throat if I'd been an assassin."

I turned a look on Miles that said, *Is this guy for real?*

Miles replied with a lift of his eyebrow and a small, amused quirk of his lips.

Steele unzipped the last pocket of my pack. "Where's your paracord?"

Paracord, an essential survival item for hikers due to its versatility, had been on his supply list, but I would have brought it anyway. I wore it woven into a bracelet on my wrist because, in an emergency situation, that was one thing you didn't want to go searching through your pack for. I pushed up the sleeve of my jacket to show him.

He did not seem impressed. "Waterproof matches?"

I unzipped the pouch inside my jacket. Again, waterproof matches were not something you wanted to take a chance on losing.

"Flashlight?"

I showed him the mini-flashlight securely fastened to my belt, although he surely had already seen it when I unzipped my jacket. Without another word, he zipped up my pack and tossed it to me, hard enough to make me stagger backward. No doubt he'd hoped to knock me down. I heard Miles draw a sharp breath, but I spoke before he could. Sometimes he forgets I hardly ever need defending.

"Aren't you going to search his pack?" I slipped on

the straps of my pack and nodded toward Miles.

"Last I heard," replied Steele, "Mr. Young wasn't planning on taking a half-dozen people into the wilderness on nothing but his own say-so."

I had no idea what he meant by that, so I did not reply.

Miles picked up his own pack and put it on. "Did you come to lead us in?" he asked, trying for a neutral tone.

"No," replied Steele. "I came to clear the trail for the others."

"We did a lot of that ourselves on the way up."

"So I saw."

I wondered how long this guy had been following us.

He turned and started back up the trail. "You can follow me in if you want. It's not far, but it's mostly uphill. Don't feel you have to try to keep up."

I strapped on Cisco's saddlebags and clipped his leash to my belt, debating whether it would be better to let the self-important Mr. Steele get well ahead before we started out. When I looked at Miles, I could tell he was thinking the same thing.

Then Steele spoke, not even glancing back to see if we were following. "Dogs are a menace and a handicap in the wilderness. They chase game. They use up resources—food, water—that you need to survive. They pull your focus. They give away your position to predators, human and animal. And that one..." He jerked his head backward toward Cisco. "A golden retriever is not even a protection dog, it's a house pet.

Totally worthless out here."

My back teeth clenched, and I sucked in a breath. "Cisco," I said coolly, "is not a house pet. He's a highly trained tracking dog, certified in wilderness search and rescue. He's had over two-dozen verified saves in the past three years. That's hardly worthless."

"Good for him." Steele slashed at a low-hanging branch with his knife, and it fell out of the way.

My nostrils flared and I compressed my lips against hasty words. Finally, when he was far enough ahead to be just out of hearing, I muttered, "What's his problem?"

Miles fastened the buckles of his backpack. "An unfortunate and increasingly common condition known as Jackass Syndrome. Don't let it bother you. I've known guys like him before. They're almost always the best at what they do. But then they'd have to be, to get away with treating everybody else like crap. I'll talk to him."

"Don't bother," I replied, scowling. "I can handle it."

He winked at me. "Do you want me to hold on to Cisco while you go beat him up, sugar?"

Of course, he was teasing, but I didn't hesitate. "Yeah," I said. I unclipped Cisco's leash and thrust it into Miles's hand, then strode forward, double-paced, to catch up to Steele.

I reached him just as the trail widened enough for us to walk side by side. He neither slowed his pace nor glanced my way to acknowledge my presence. I was breathing hard from the hasty ascent, which I thought put me at a disadvantage, so I tried to control my breath before I spoke.

"Listen," I said. "I don't know what you've got against me, but we're going to be working together and there's no point in getting off on the wrong foot. I know you're the expert here, and I'm sure I can learn a lot from you. But I bring plenty to the table, too. If I didn't, I wouldn't be here. I think this whole week will go a lot smoother if we start over by showing each other a little mutual respect."

All things considered, I think that was a very generous speech. Noble, even. I should have at least received credit for the effort. He didn't acknowledge it with so much as a nod.

His voice was flat, almost disinterested, as he said, "I don't have anything against you, Miss Stockton. I don't know you. Not sure I even want to. And we are not working together. You're here because the insurance company requires two wilderness experts on site, and your boyfriend somehow managed to convince them you are one. I don't need you to respect me or help me. I just need you to stay out of my way. And," he added pointedly, "try not to be a liability."

Whatever inclination I had toward being reasonable disappeared in a flash of temper. I could feel it flaring in my eyes and burning in my cheeks. I swung in front of him, stopping his forward motion, standing still. "For your information, I've been hiking the Smoky Mountain wilderness all my life. I'm trained in free climbing, abseiling, and belay. I'm certified in high mountain rescue and emergency first aid. I've worked for the forest service as a guide and a consultant. This is *not* my first wilderness expedition, and I am *not* a liability."

His demeanor remained unchanged. "Look, lady," he said.

I *hate* it when people call me lady.

"I don't mean to insult you or your pup," he went on, his voice a cold pretense of patience. "But I looked you up. You're a dog trainer, plain and simple. I'm sure you're very good at what you do. But I've got less than a week to teach a bunch of soft-bellied city folks how to survive in situations they can't even picture in their worst nightmares, and if I fail some of them are going to die. Period. I don't have time to be nice about it, and I sure as hell don't have time to worry about hurting your feelings. Because, let's face it, without your dog you're just another tourist wandering around the woods. And that, believe me, is the last thing I need."

I didn't know what to say to that. He stepped around me, moving ahead with those long, forceful strides, and I let him go.

Miles and Cisco came up beside me. "Everything okay?" Miles asked.

I frowned after Steele, who was already well ahead of us. "Not even close," I said.

At Miles's quizzically lifted eyebrow, I shrugged and retrieved Cisco's leash. "Jackass Syndrome," I explained. "No cure."

We followed Steele at our own pace, not trying or wanting to keep up with him. Steele's words had stung, and I couldn't get them out of my mind. Worse, I couldn't help wondering whether he was right.

Maybe I was out of my depth. Maybe I didn't belong here.

Moreover, about twenty minutes up the trail, the sky began to darken with a film of heavy gray clouds that blotted out the sun and cast the ground beneath our feet into cold, gloomy shadow. It looked as though the storm hadn't passed, after all.

CHAPTER EIGHT

J essup was convinced that the internet had made humans stupid. Not just because of the endless supply of drivel and lies it spewed forth which stole people's time and fixed their focus on a deliberate effort to become stupid, but because of its actual truths. Why bother to remember the creek crossings, the hidden trails, the old road shortcuts, when you could just pull up a map from Google Earth and see them in real time? Why learn to cut for sign when a drone or a satellite photo could find your prey in an instant? Why use your brain and your senses to read the weather when the tap of an icon could deliver the ten-day forecast at absolutely no charge? People were even using the internet to identify birdsong and species of flora, uploading a photo to determine whether a plant was edible or poisonous instead of imprinting that very same information deep in their consciousness, as one naturally did when a mistake could mean the difference between life and death. Whole parts of the human brain were dying from misuse, and what people didn't realize was that when one part of the brain began to fade—even if it was a part you thought you didn't need anymore—the whole human became stupider.

This was why, Jessup believed, he was smarter than the average twenty-first-century man. He remembered every trail he had ever taken, every stream he had ever crossed. He remembered where the bears denned in winter and where the wildcats liked to hunt. He remembered where he had left every single body or body part he'd ever disposed of. His eyes were sharp, his senses alert, his reflexes instantaneous. The brain was his most important survival tool.

He hadn't been to the Hidden Lodge area of the Tennessee Smoky Mountains in over twenty years, but he remembered every trail, ridge, cove, and stream. That was the beauty of the wilderness: it was, at its heart, unchanging. He had taken two young women from there between 1998 and 2002, enjoyed them each for a couple of weeks, and then disposed of them in the deep woods off one of the private-use trails near Hidden Lodge. The last one hadn't been found for over three years, and both were in far too advanced a state of decomposition for identification. It was a good place for disposal, which was one of the reasons he had returned here.

It was always a good idea to dispose of the remains as far away from the kill site as possible, and he tried to do so whenever practical. This part of the Smokies was easily fifty miles from the place Jessup had left the Ringgolds' RV, and a good deal farther than that from her husband's remains. When the last pieces of her were found, if they were found at all, the connection between two missing retirees would be extremely difficult to make.

Hidden Lodge was an old hunting camp set on the edge of Great Smoky Mountains National Park, used in the summertime for things like Boy Scout retreats and folk-art festivals. This time of year it was closed down and locked up, with no one scheduled to check on it until spring. But there were always a few nonperishables left to winter-over in mouse-proof metal boxes: paper goods, powdered milk, sugar, flour, dehydrated soup. With winter coming on, Jessup, like all predators, was aware of the need to fatten up his stores. That was the other reason he had decided on a route that took him into this deserted part of the forest.

That was why he was surprised—and disappointed—to meet a park service jeep as he drove along the old service road that looped behind the lodge and that was generally used for nothing other than to supply the building. He lifted his hand to her in a friendly way and she did the same to him, although he could see she was surprised to find someone out here this time of year as well. Was she going to close up the place? Performing one last inspection before winterizing? It would be worth checking out later tonight.

Meantime, his plans were disrupted and that was mildly annoying. But he would adjust. Everyone knew one of the primary keys to survival was the ability to adapt.

CHAPTER NINE

The lodge was a rectangular log structure with a fairly new-looking green metal roof and a covered porch along the front. Almost-clear smoke shimmered from each of the building's two chimneys, which meant someone had built high-temperature fires with well-seasoned wood inside. By then, the sun had been behind the clouds long enough to cause a noticeable drop in temperature, and I was looking forward to warming my hands in front of a good fire.

We passed a metal building with a padlocked garage door set a short distance away from the lodge which I assumed was a maintenance shed. A lean-to next to it held what appeared to be a couple of cords of split firewood. Behind the main building were two green lap-sided buildings of the kind you see in park campgrounds everywhere, one marked "Restrooms" and the other marked "Showers." In front of the building was a sturdy park grill and a firepit with a circular stone seating area surrounding it. All of this stood in the middle of a wilderness of spruce and pine trees and absolutely nothing else.

A woman in a park ranger uniform waited on the porch as we approached. She wore a billed hat and the name tag on her jacket, I saw as I grew closer, read "Meg Oakley." Cisco perked up when he saw her and bounded up the three steps ahead of us, almost reaching the end of his expandable bungee leash. I was relieved to see the woman wasn't a dog-hater when she got down on one knee and ruffled Cisco's ears, declaring, "Well, look at you, handsome! What a good dog!"

Cisco knew a cue when he saw one and took her friendliness as an invitation for a hug. He reared up on his haunches, grinning happily, and placed both of his muddy paws on her shoulders.

"Cisco, off!" I cried, hurrying forward. "I'm so sorry!" I told the woman. "He's very, um, friendly."

Fortunately, she was a good sport about it, laughing as she got to her feet and tried without much success to brush the paw prints off her uniform jacket. "Don't worry about it," she said. "I think I asked for that one."

I introduced myself and Cisco and fished a treat from my pocket to lure Cisco back to my side. "I like a dog who carries his own weight," she responded, grinning as she indicated Cisco's backpack. She offered her hand to me. Her nails were painted bright pink, which probably wasn't regulation. "Meg Oakley, lodge manager." She turned to Miles. "You must be Mr. Young. Welcome to Hidden Lodge."

They shook hands and Miles glanced around. "Where's Mr. Steele?"

"I believe he's out exploring," she replied, moving toward the door. "But I'll show you around."

I can't express how glad I was to hear that Mr. Rick Steele was not on the premises.

The interior of the lodge revealed a big keeping room—a combination kitchen, dining, and living room—that was heated to a comfortable temperature by a wood-burning stove on the central wall. The furniture was simple but sturdy—a couple of sofas, some low wooden chairs with thick cushions, and braided cotton rugs. A long trestle table divided the kitchen from the living area. Meg led us to the kitchen first.

"You're all stocked up for nine people, five days, as requested," she said. She glanced at me with a flicker of concern. "We didn't know about the dog."

"Cisco is self-sufficient," I assured her and tugged at one of his ears. He looked up at me with a grin and then started sniffing the floor for crumbs.

She opened the freezer door to reveal a stack of foil casserole pans. "High-calorie, nutrient-dense dinners," she said. "Heat at 350 for thirty minutes." She opened the refrigerator door on a collection of prepackaged salads, cold cuts, and breads. The cupboards were stacked with canned soups, fruit cocktail, instant oatmeal, shelf-stable milk, and other nonperishables. "You'll obviously do your own cooking and cleaning," she said. "Maid service isn't until the end of your stay. The building is heated completely with wood. You probably saw the woodshed on your way in. Potable water comes from a well, and hot water is solar-heated from a fifty-gallon tank." She grinned at me. "That means it's first-come, first-serve for a hot shower. The stove is propane. A generator runs the lights, kitchen appliances, and the well pump."

Miles looked around approvingly. "All in all, not as bad as I expected."

There was a big metal urn on the countertop that smelled of coffee; Miles took a cup from the stack beside it and filled it with steaming black brew. He glanced at me inquisitively and I shook my head. "Maybe later," I said. I was thinking about that hot shower before the others got here, and how good it would feel to get out of my grungy hiking clothes and into soft, clean sweats.

Meg led the way from the kitchen. "The bunk room sleeps ten," she said. She opened a door off the living area onto a cold corridor that was paneled in dark logs. We followed her a few steps down that hallway to another door on the right. This one opened onto a large dorm space that was heated by another wood-burning stove. Two windows let in a haze of cloudy light. The bare-mattressed cots were lined up along the two walls adjacent to the stove, with a footlocker at the end of each bed. A small wooden table containing a battery-operated lamp sat between each of the cots.

I unsnapped the buckles of my pack and gratefully dumped it on the nearest cot. Miles let his pack drop onto the cot next to mine while I unbuckled Cisco's saddlebags.

"Home sweet home," Miles said and took a sip of his coffee.

"So that's the grand tour," Meg said. "There's another bedroom across the hall, much smaller of course, but I believe it's already taken by Mr. Steele. Next to it is a small storage and radio room. Exits and rules for occupancy are clearly posted." She gestured to the exit sign over the door and the framed notice beside the door. "I understand the others will be arriving later, but if you're set here, I'm going to take off. I'm starting a two-week leave tomorrow," she explained, which I thought probably explained the pink nails, "and I want to check a couple of the trails before I leave."

Miles assured her we could handle it from here, and I said, "Are there regular patrols or anything? I mean, we're pretty isolated out here, and the ranger station is on the other side of the mountain."

She looked mildly puzzled by the question. "That's why most people come here. Someone will be by to close the place up after you leave, but until then I don't expect you'll see another soul." She gave me a reassuring smile. "There's a radio in case of emergency, but no one has ever needed it."

I gave her a quick thumbs-up. "Sounds great," I said. "Just curious. Have a good vacation."

As soon as she left, I unclipped Cisco's leash from my belt and he scampered off to explore, toenails clicking on the old wood floors. Since we kept the door to the dorm closed to conserve heat, there wasn't much for him to explore, but he made the best of it, circling the room with his nose to the floor, checking under beds and around the footlockers, pausing to give the woodpile beside the stove a thorough examination. While he was thus engaged, I sat down on my bunk and started to unlace my boots.

Then I paused, remembering something. "Nine," I said.

Miles had his phone out, no doubt double-checking for internet. "What's that, babe?"

"You, me, and Steele," I said. "That's three. Five people coming on the shuttle, right? That's eight. But the ranger said we were provisioned for nine. So who's the ninth person?"

"Huh." Miles's attention was still on his phone, despite the lack of internet or cell service. "Couldn't say." He put his phone away and picked up his coffee cup again. "I think I saw popcorn in one of those cabinets. What do you say, Cisco, you want to check it out?"

People who think dogs don't understand English clearly don't speak English to their dogs. At the words "popcorn" and "Cisco," my faithful companion bounded over to Miles, ready to follow him anywhere.

They went off to the kitchen, but I remained where I was, taking my time gathering up my shower things while I assessed my surroundings. That's something that anyone who's spent any time in the wilderness does automatically, and even though I wasn't exactly in the wilderness inside the lodge, the same instincts applied. Where were the exits? What did we need for comfort, necessity, and survival, and how far away were those things? What were the dangers? —and in this particular case, I meant dangers for dogs. Exposed wires? Mousetraps or poisons? Cabinets without locks? Silly, maybe. But, like I said, it was instinct.

Besides, there was something about the place—and this is something I would not admit, even to Miles —that spooked me a little. Completely isolated. No phone. No internet. No patrols. A bunch of strangers, one of whom might very well be engaged in corporate espionage. I'd seen that movie. And in circumstances like that, you can't be too careful.

If only I had known what the circumstances really were, I wouldn't have felt silly at all.

CHAPTER TEN

The ninth person turned out to be Ian Wharton, an observer from Tanner-Fielding International, the insurance underwriter who would be responsible for certifying the corporate execs as fit for duty—or at least, fit for a discounted rate—after they completed the course. He was a smallish, wiry man in glasses and thinning red hair who was at the head of the pack of straggling hikers who made their way toward the lodge. Cisco, Miles, and I waited for them on the covered porch, protected in our sweaters and down vests from the cold mist of rain that had begun about an hour earlier. Wharton strode forward, introduced himself, and shook Miles's hand energetically. Despite his frail appearance, he would appear to be in better shape than any of them.

"Quite a hike for a bunch of city folks," he observed jovially. "We'll all sleep good tonight, I'll tell you."

"I doubt that," I said. "You haven't seen the bunks yet." I extended my hand. "Raine Stockton. And this is my dog, Cisco."

"Right." He took my hand in a bone-crushing grip and pumped it once. "The local wilderness expert. I was copied on the e-mail last night. Good for you, Young, for finding her on such short notice. And your tracking dog, right? Good idea, bringing him along. We can learn a lot from dogs."

Now *that* was the way Cisco and I should have been greeted by Mr. Know-It-All Steele, and I told Miles so with a look while Ian Wharton bent to scratch Cisco's chin.

Cisco was, of course, in ecstasy as one by one the rest of the group trooped up the steps, damp and miserable and exhausted. He wagged his tail so hard he almost threw himself off balance as he went from one to the other of them, hearing their complaints turn into surprised exclamations of, "Hey, whose dog?" and "What a pretty boy!" as they bent to pet him. There's nothing like a golden retriever to brighten even the dampest spirits.

Unfortunately, those bright spirits quickly turned to annoyance as Cisco's enthusiasm increased. I heard a shout of, "Hey!" and turned to see Cisco happily dragging someone's backpack across the porch by the strap. I caught his collar and apologized as I quickly returned the pack to its owner, but the recipient did not look too happy as he tried to brush the dog slobber off the strap of his pack. I scowled a reprimand to Cisco and pulled him into a sharp heel position at my knee. He grinned up at me, completely unrepentant.

Rick Steele brought up the rear, having apparently gone down the trail to make sure everyone arrived safely. Points for him. Before Miles or I could say anything, Steele announced, "Okay, people, listen up. Hot coffee and a warm fire inside. Stow your gear in the bunk room and get into dry clothes. Assemble in the keeping room in ten minutes."

A few explicit looks were exchanged between the executives as Steele pushed past them to go inside. These were people who were accustomed to giving orders, not taking them, and they very likely might have made that clear had not Miles been standing there, watching them with an amused look on his face.

One of the men straightened up from petting Cisco—not the same one, I should point out, whose backpack Cisco had stolen—and looked at Miles. He was a good-looking man of about forty with thick, expensively barbered blond hair, manicured nails, and navy-blue eyes. Everything about him said Big City, but he also struck me as the kind of man who could hold the attention of a room full of people just by standing there and looking at them, much like Miles could. He said, "So, boss. We were all wondering on the way up…" He glanced around casually at the others. "What did we do to piss you off?"

Miles grinned and pushed open the door, gesturing them all inside. Naturally, Cisco wriggled in first. "Good to see you, Parker. And this week, you've only got one boss, and it's not me." He inclined his head toward Steele, who had already made his way to the coffee urn in the kitchen. "Raine, this is Parker Sandoval. We were in the military together."

Parker grinned back and shook my hand. "He was my boss then, too. We got a group text about a last-minute personnel sub. Wilderness guide, right? Didn't expect you to be so cute."

He said it in such a way that it would have been impossible to take offense, even if I'd been so inclined. I was about to say something cute in response, but Miles raised his voice as everybody clattered inside, closing the door behind them. "Everybody, quick introductions. This is Raine Stockton, wilderness expert. The dog is Cisco, also a wilderness and tracking expert. Don't feed him without permission."

He went around the room and introduced the others: BJ Valentine was a fit-looking, attractive woman with a chin-length honey-colored bob that had somehow remained smooth and bouncy despite the rain. Maxine Hodges, the only other woman, was plumper, ruddy-faced, dark-haired, and put-out-looking. Theo Carter, one of the men who had flown in from Italy, was probably in his late fifties, barrel-chested and round-shouldered. He groaned as he lowered his backpack to the floor. He looked jet-lagged and miserable. I worried about him being able to complete another hike of any distance and hoped Steele had built recovery time into his schedule. His counterpart, Reed Barnes, was the one on whom Cisco had made such a poor first impression. He looked as though he had spent his time in Italy on the Riveria. He was golden-tanned and silver-haired, with broad shoulders and a big, booming voice, and by the skeptical looks he tossed Cisco I could tell he was not the kind to overlook a slight. Which one of them, I wondered, did Miles suspect? And which, if any, was capable of betraying him?

They all greeted me with perfunctory politeness until Miles added, "In the interest of full disclosure, and so that Parker doesn't continue to embarrass himself, Raine is also my fiancée."

I would have preferred that Miles not do that—this was a job, after all—but I suppose in a group this small it was inevitable. There were a few curious, surprised looks and exclamations of "Congratulations!" as the pleased-to-meet-you smiles grew broader.

Parker pulled an expression of exaggerated disappointment and said, "Damn. And I was just about to ask if she had dinner plans." He clapped Miles on the shoulder with a grin. "Good on you, man. I hadn't heard."

Reed Barnes's big voice carried as he declared to Miles, "Well, now it makes more sense! I wondered why you'd cancel Switzerland for"—he gestured around the room with a grimace of mild distaste—"this."

BJ, the pretty one, looked me over studiously, then turned back to Miles. She said thoughtfully, "Miles Young, you are a complicated man."

"So I am," he agreed and rested his hand lightly on my back.

It was an affectionate gesture, not a possessive one, but it made BJ smile. "All right, then," she said. She bent down to pick up her pack by the strap. "Let's go find this so-called bunk room. There's turn-down service, I presume?"

I waited until they had all shuffled down the corridor toward the bunk room, talking and joking wearily among themselves, to glance up at Miles and inquire, "Ex?"

"BJ, you mean?" He shrugged. "Very ex." He lifted an eyebrow at me. "That's not a problem, is it?"

I replied, "As long as she doesn't feed my dog without permission, it isn't."

I had decided long ago it was pointless to be jealous of Miles. He was rich, smart, funny, good looking, and a heck of a dancer. He had been on the cover of a magazine as "Atlanta's Most Eligible Bachelor." He could have any woman he wanted, yet he chose to be with me. When—or if—he chose not to be with me, there would be nothing I could do to change things. In the meantime, with so many other things in the world that were out of my control, that was one thing I refused to worry about.

He chuckled and kissed my hair. "I'm going to bring in more firewood."

"I'll take Cisco out and meet you back here," I said.

I had left Cisco's leash on my bunk, and I made my way back to retrieve it. Cisco, naturally, had raced ahead after the others, and before I even reached the bunk room I heard a squeal and a cry, "Come back with that!"

I arrived to see Cisco standing atop Max's bunk next to her open backpack, her bra in his mouth. She tried to tug it away from him, which of course made him only more excited about the game. She gave a cry of dismay as he leapt off the bunk and raced around the room, carrying the pretty aqua undergarment like a banner while everyone else looked on, laughing.

I shouted, "Cisco, halt! Here!"

He skidded to a stop, turned, and pranced back to me. I held out my hand and he dropped his prize, now damp and wrinkled, into it. I returned the bra to Max apologetically. It was satin and lacey with heavy underwire, completely impractical for the week ahead. I had brought nothing but sports bras.

"I'm so sorry," I said. "He gets a little excited sometimes."

Max gave me an unhappy look and did not reply as she turned to stuff the bra back into her backpack. Parker, who was sitting on his bunk tugging off his boots, stopped chuckling abruptly when Cisco dashed over and snatched up the dry pair of socks he had pulled out of his backpack.

Some people might say Cisco has terrible manners for a working dog. To those people, I would reply: Walk a mile in my shoes. Cisco's high energy, independence, and enthusiasm are exactly what *make* him a great working dog, and I wouldn't trade those qualities for all the obedience ribbons in dogdom. Although, at moments like these, I would have traded him for a sweet, lumbering, drooling, low-energy Newfoundland in a heartbeat.

To be perfectly fair, though, Cisco hadn't, for all practical purposes, been out of the house in months. Of course he was excited. Of course he had forgotten a few manners. What more could I expect from him?

This time I caught Cisco before he had made half a circuit around the room. He dropped the socks on command—too little, too late, some might say—and I didn't bother to apologize as I returned them to Parker. To do so felt redundant.

I held Cisco's collar until I got his leash on and marched him out of the room. "Way to make an impression," I muttered to him, but he was completely oblivious.

It was going to be a long week.

CHAPTER ELEVEN

Jessup would never know what brought the park ranger so far from the access road onto private land, midway down a trail that no one ever used. It was for those reasons that he had chosen this spot. After passing the ranger in her jeep, Jessup had continued down the service road about a mile, then pulled into the woods far enough that the truck would not be visible from the road. This placed him in familiar territory, which was both good and bad. It was good because his knowledge of the terrain would allow him to be in and out quickly. It was bad because it meant breaking one of his cardinal rules for escaping detection: avoid patterns. He had left two bodies here before, decades ago. He was about to leave a third.

But of course, out here in the wilderness without smartphones or surveillance cameras, where even satellites had a hard time getting an accurate view, patterns were a good deal more difficult to detect than they might have been otherwise. The average law enforcement officer's brain, like that of the average human, had grown dumber over the years as reliance on modern technology increased. This was Jessup's advantage.

He removed the final remains of Mary Ringgold, wrapped in a black plastic trash bag that dripped ice water, from the cooler and slung the bag over his shoulder. He hiked half a mile down the rutted, brush-lined road when he spotted the park service jeep, empty, pulled off the road and practically indiscernible about ten feet into the woods on a half-hidden trail. He looked around, checked the signs, and saw boot prints in the mud headed north. He continued south, determined to avoid an encounter if he could. He could handle trouble if it came his way, but he didn't seek it out.

Less than a mile farther on he came upon the old, seldom-used trail he remembered from years ago. It led to the lodge, which was why he chose it. After he finished his final business with Mary Ringgold, he would hike down to the lodge and check it out. If all was as he expected it to be, he would help himself to the provisions there and be on his way. Otherwise... he would adapt.

He was required to adapt sooner than he expected when he parted the rhododendron thicket which he intended to be the final resting place of what remained of Mary Ringgold and saw the park ranger climbing the up bank directly opposite him just across the trail. He took a step back, but too late. She looked startled when she saw him. "Oh, hi," she said, stepping back onto the trail. "You must be with the group from the lodge."

There was a group at the lodge. Good intel. He smiled and lowered the trash bag carefully to the ground. "Afternoon," he said. "Just doing a little exploring."

A slight flicker in her eyes told him she didn't quite believe him. She jerked a thumb over her shoulder toward the bank she'd just climbed. "Someone dumped a whole bunch of soda cans and stuff down there." She looked at the trash bag at his feet suspiciously. "You weren't planning to do anything like that, were you? Because you know it's illegal."

"Yes, ma'am, I know," he assured her, still smiling.

She looked deliberately at the trash bag. "Do you mind if I ask what's in that bag?"

"Not at all." He picked up the bag and walked toward her. "Have a look if you want."

The smell was intense, and it reached her before he did. She took a step back, standing on the edge of the bank. He opened the bag to show her the contents.

Jessup had a variety of weapons: hunting knives, long guns, pistols. The crossbow was his favorite for wilderness hunting. It was quick, accurate, and silent. It was important to have the right tool for the job. On this particular expedition, he carried two primary weapons, a bowie knife in a scabbard at his waist, and a .22 pistol in a back holster. Before the ranger could even scream, the minute she raised her horrified gaze from the contents of the plastic trash bag to Jessup's face, he shot her through the eye with the .22. It was quick, deadly, and neat. The sound was like the cracking of a limb on a windy afternoon, and she fell backward down the bank from which she had come.

When faced with the unexpected in the wilderness, whether it was an injury, a wrong turn that left them lost, a wild animal encounter, or an accident that ruined all their supplies, the average person made one simple, often deadly mistake: they panicked. This development was definitely unexpected. But Jessup had survived far too long in the wilderness to panic.

Stop.

He holstered his weapon and sat on his haunches.

He thought the situation over.

He carefully observed his surroundings and weighed his options.

He made a plan.

And then he got to work.

CHAPTER TWELVE

I took Cisco out for a brief toilet break, and when I returned everyone was milling around the kitchen area, filling their coffee cups, finding a place at the long table where Steele had set up a whiteboard. On the board was written the familiar mnemonic for survival:

Sit
Think
Observe
Plan

From this I gathered class was about to begin. There were pens and notebooks in front of each chair, and I took a seat toward the middle of the table, instructing Cisco to lie down under the table near my feet. This would, I knew, be a test of his self-control, given all the exciting new people who—he was convinced—were eager to pet him. In fact, this entire week would be a test for him and, I supposed, for me. This was definitely not our usual crowd.

BJ put her coffee mug on the table and sat next to me. Cisco started to scramble to his feet to greet her but before he could I gave his leash a sharp tug and he slid back down to his belly again. As always, the best defense is an offense when it comes to reminding your dog of his obedience commands.

BJ ran her fingers lightly over her face, which I couldn't help noticing was complete with mascara, blush, and lip gloss. She stifled a groan and said, "My skin is dry enough to crack open. I can't believe I forgot to pack my face cream. You don't have any moisturizer, do you?"

I said, "Sorry," even as I wondered what kind of person packed face cream on a wilderness excursion. "I don't use it."

"Really?" She studied my face with a mixture of surprise and curiosity. "Your skin is beautiful."

"Oh," I said, a little taken aback. "Thanks." I glanced away and smoothed a curl of hair behind my ear self-consciously.

She picked up her coffee cup. "So, how did you and Miles meet?"

I was about to tell her, but Theo Carter pulled out the chair on the other side of me and said, "Where's your pup?"

Cisco stood up so excitedly that he bumped his head on the table. I corrected him with another tug on the leash and a sharp, "Ank!" of reprimand. Cisco lay back down again. I suppose that answered Theo's question because he leaned around me to ask BJ, "Did you get the proposal on the Pendleton project?"

Rick Steele said loudly, "Okay, people, find a seat and settle down. Let's get to work."

Max, the only other woman in the group, slid into a chair opposite us and sat down heavily. "Co-ed dorms," she remarked. "I feel like I'm back at summer camp."

"Your summer camp sounds like a lot more fun than mine," BJ said. "And how'd you like those 700-thread-count organic sheets?"

"If I'd known we were supposed to bring our own linens," replied Max, stirring her coffee, "I would have *brought* my own linens. And what are we supposed to do for towels?"

I started to point out that one quick-dry towel had been on the supply list, and their sleeping bags would do just fine for bed linens, but just then Steele said, "Welcome to Hidden Lodge."

People ended their conversations and turned their attention to him. Miles put a mug of coffee in front of me—heavy on the cream, two sugars, just the way I liked it—and I smiled my thanks at him. I couldn't help noticing, out of the corner of my eye, the way BJ tracked the exchange. He went around the table to sit opposite me. I heard Cisco's tail start to thump in greeting and I tightened his leash.

"There is no room service, no internet, no bar, and no gym," Steele went on. "Firewood is in the shed at the top of the drive. I advise you to lay in a good supply before nightfall. You will divide KP duty among yourselves. There is a limited supply of hot water, so the shower schedule will be as follows: Saturday, Monday, Wednesday, and Friday, ladies from 5:30 a.m. to 6:00 a.m., gents from 5:30 p.m. to 6:00 p.m. Sunday, Tuesday, and Thursday, the schedule is reversed."

After one quick look at Steele to make sure he was serious, the attendees started quickly scribbling on their pads. I was glad I'd already showered.

"Your day will begin at sunrise and end at sunset," Steele went on. "You will work hard and sleep hard. You've all been medically cleared for the physical activities involved, so I don't want to hear any whining."

I noticed a few frowns of concern that were quickly hidden, and I felt a little sorry for them. Barnes was in his late fifties and Max was clearly no marathon runner. Theo Carter was more of a wet-noodle type than a prime physical specimen, and none of them had counted on having to pass a fitness test if that's what Steele had in mind. I personally thought the fact that they'd managed the hike in was enough to prove their capabilities in that arena.

Steele looked around the group, his gaze resting on each one separately, sizing them up. Then he said, "A lot of you are wondering why I chose this place. I know it's not the Mariott conference room you're probably used to. That's exactly the point. This is not a game. If you fall in a creek, you *will* get hypothermia. If you put your hand in a bear trap, you will lose it. Out here you're at least a day's walk from the outside world. No phones, no Urgent Care, no 911. Help is not coming. I want you to let that sink in for a minute. Help. Is. Not. Coming."

His words were chilling, but I respected him for saying them. How many times have I said the same thing about careless tourists who treat the National Forest like a theme park in which some perky hostess in a uniform is always standing by to come to their aid? I could tell by the quick, uneasy looks that were exchanged that this was not exactly the experience any of them had prepared for.

Of course, if I had been running the show, I might have mentioned the emergency radio and the satellite phone, but that's just me. I got his point.

He said, "That, and the words written on this board here...." He gestured to the whiteboard. "... are the two most important things you will ever learn about wilderness survival. Survival begins in the mind. Survival begins with self-reliance. The deadliest mistake people make in an emergency situation is to panic. Stop moving. Think. Observe your surroundings. Make a plan. And know that whether you live or die is dependent on the choices you make. Help is not coming.

"That having been said," Steele went on, "keep your eyes and ears open, your senses alert, your mind working at all times. Remember what you're about to learn. Do what you're told. This place is the closest I could come to simulating the kind of stress you'll be under in a real wilderness survival situation. Use it. Test yourself. You'll be pushed to your breaking point, but you probably won't die. Not here, at least, and not on my watch."

He let the heavy silence that followed his words settle over the group for a minute, and then he turned to Miles. "I believe Mr. Young wants to say a few words." He sat down at the head of the table.

The tension around the table was palpable, and Miles eased it with a small smile and a lift of his coffee cup. "Let's make that 'definitely,'" he said. "You *definitely* won't die here. We've got enough insurance problems as it is."

There were a few chuckles and Ian Wharton, the insurance guy who'd been so nice to Cisco, smiled and returned Miles's salute with his own coffee cup. People relaxed in their chairs.

Miles said, "This is a different kind of retreat than most of you are used to. It's not about team building or brainstorming. No one is judging you or watching your performance. All I care about—all Mr. Steele cares about, and Mr. Wharton and Ms. Stockton—is your safety. That's why we're here. You are some of the most valuable members of my team. Consequently, you are entrusted with the most responsibility, and that often means you take the most risks, both professionally and personally. If somebody has to scout out a new location or troubleshoot a manufacturing problem or negotiate a contract in one of the world's hotspots, chances are it will be one of you. And yes, you get all the State Department alerts. You travel with security and local guides. You also know that in most of these countries, an American hostage is worth more than any security team gets paid, and most of the local guides are working for the same corrupt governments that trade hostages for arms on a daily basis. So there's that."

My throat felt a little dry as I listened to him. I had always pictured Miles living it up in resort hotels with glassed-in spas and fifty-dollar cocktails when he traveled abroad, and maybe he did. Probably he did. But now my vision widened to include bulletproof cars and turbaned drivers who carried assault weapons under their robes. I'd just never thought about it before.

Miles paused to take a sip of his coffee. "Three years ago, a plane carrying 113 passengers went down in the Balkan Mountains. A dozen people survived the impact. Four were American executives on their way to oversee the building of a new hotel in Montenegro. It took rescuers two weeks to reach them. By the time they did, all four Americans were dead of exposure, dehydration and wounds sustained unrelated to the crash. You probably remember their names: Jack Boston, Ralph Carney, Lee Sun Yoo, Dave Washington. They worked with some of the same people you do, and I believe to this day their deaths could have been prevented if they'd had the same kind of training you're about to get."

A moment of respectful, if painful, silence gripped the group. Miles's eyes were lowered, but I couldn't help staring at him. I'd never known. I was starting to think there was a lot about Miles I didn't know.

Miles looked around the group again. "Some of

you remember Scott Livingston. He spent two years in a Russian prison before negotiators from Baylor Industries were able to secure his release. And of course, we all know what happened to Brett Barkley last year on what was supposed to be a routine trip to Venezuela." He leaned back in his chair, hands cradling his cup against his chest, his mild gray gaze moving over them. "So, look. Chances are you'll never need what you're about to learn this week. I hope to God you don't. But you are worth it to me and to the company to make sure you have the resources you need to take care of yourselves in case the unexpected happens. I can't afford to lose you." One by one he looked at them. "Any of you."

After a moment, Miles nodded at Steele, turning the meeting back over to him. Cisco, bored, yawned loudly under the table. A few people, glad for the chance to lighten the mood, smiled. Steele did not.

"Okay," Steele said, "here's the situation. You're in a hotel room in an environment much like this —isolated, surrounded by woods, temperature not much above freezing at night. You are about to be taken prisoner by hostile forces. Assuming you're already wearing clothing appropriate for the climate, you have thirty seconds to grab three items that will help you survive. These must be items that you brought with you, or that are readily found in your room. We'll go around the table. Tell me what you'd take and why."

He turned to Theo Carter, who was sitting to his right. Theo looked uncertain. "Well, um…"

"Thirty seconds," Steele reminded him.

"Well," said Theo. "Okay. I'd grab my phone to call an Uber to get me the hell out of there." A few chuckles greeted that. He added, "My wallet, because it has my credit cards and ID, and my passport because I'll need it to get home."

Steele did not comment. He just made a note on the pad in front of him and nodded to the next person, who happened to be me.

I said, "I'd grab my multitool. I keep it in my purse or my backpack all the time. It has a hammer, a saw, a knife, a fire starter, a screwdriver, pliers, scissors, a safety whistle, and five other tools and it folds small enough to fit in my pocket. I'd take tampons." This seemed to amuse some and confuse others until I explained, "They can be used to filter water, or pack a wound, as a torch when soaked in pine sap, or as tinder for a fire. They're lightweight, easy to carry, and sanitary supplies are not likely to be confiscated if you're taken captive. And," I concluded, "I'd take my dog because if I'm moving through an unfamiliar wilderness area, he's my best chance of getting out alive."

I have to admit, the looks of admiration that went around the table did a lot for my ego, as did Miles's wink of encouragement. Everyone was catching on to the game now, and BJ said, after only a moment's thought, "Hand sanitizer. It can be used as an antiseptic for wounds and the alcohol will burn like crazy when you're trying to get a fire started. The hand mirror from my purse, for signaling and starting a fire. The sewing kit from the hotel bathroom. There are over a thousand feet of thread in those things that you can weave together and use like rope or make into a fishing line or net. There are scissors for cutting things or you can sharpen them into blades, and you can bend the needles into fishhooks."

I was impressed. But it was Parker who surprised me the most. He said without hesitation, "All the vodka and cashews in the minibar." Everyone laughed, but he was serious. "Vodka is an antiseptic and anesthetic. Mixed with stream water, it can neutralize many contaminants, and when the bottle is empty it can be used to carry and store water. It can also be used to bribe locals if the occasion arises. Cashews are high salt and high protein. Salt deprivation is a real problem in long-term survival situations and something most people don't think about until they're down with a life-threatening gut issue. I'd also take all the waste basket liners. They can be used to carry water and forage, and to line a lean-to to keep out rain and wind."

Theo said, "Um, can I change my answer?"

There were more chuckles, and Parker grinned at him. "Don't worry, buddy, I'll save some vodka for you."

My opinion of the city folks rose considerably as the exercise continued. Max thought of bringing matches, which she collected from hotel bars, and the bottle of water that was always on the bedside table— two obvious choices the rest of us had overlooked. Ian Wharton demurred, saying, "I'm just here to observe, folks. But if you want my opinion, you're doing great."

When it was Miles's turn he said, "An extra pair of socks. They can be used to bandage wounds, to collect nuts and berries you might need to stay alive, to filter water, to keep your feet warm when the socks you're wearing get wet. They can be tied together to protect your face and ears from the wind or to construct a trap for game, and if worse comes to worst, they can be unraveled for the thread to use as fishing line or rope. I'd also take a big bag of tortilla chips." By the number of smiles that went around the room, I guessed most people knew about Miles's predilection for junk food. "The fat and salt make them a good source of short-term energy, and the high oil content makes them perfect tinder for a fire. When the bag is empty you can use it to carry water. Most importantly..." His eyes met mine. "I'd take Raine Stockton, not only because of that sweet multitool she carries in her pocket..." He smiled, and indulgent chuckles went around the table. Then he added seriously, "But because a partner you can trust is the most important survival tool anybody can have."

Not that anyone ever would, but should someone ask what it was I saw in Miles, right there is the answer. Because he meant what he said and he wasn't ashamed to say it, and he did it without thought or hesitation. The emotion that welled up in me was so intense I had to look away because I could sense the eyes of the others on me, and my feelings were nobody's business but my own. And Miles's.

"All right, then." Steele scraped back his chair and

stood. "Your future instruction will be a combination of classroom and practical experience. Tomorrow is a full day. I suggest you all get some chow and hit the sack."

Max exclaimed, "Wait! Who won? Is there a prize?"

Everyone grinned except Steele. He said flatly, "Breakfast is at 0600. Don't be late." Without another word, he left the table.

The others seemed to breathe a sigh of relief when he was gone, pushing back their chairs and talking among themselves. Miles said, "You heard the man. Let's eat. I'll take the first kitchen duty."

BJ volunteered, "I'll help."

I released Cisco from his down-stay and got up from the table, hurrying after Steele. I caught up to him as he reached the front door. "Mr. Steele," I said. "You didn't tell me what you want me to do. Shouldn't we talk about tomorrow's agenda?"

He looked me over as he pulled on his jacket. His eyes came to rest on Cisco, who was wagging his tail and grinning up at him goofily, and then moved back to my face. He said, "No. If you can't figure out what you need to do, you've got no business being here."

He opened the door on a cold draft of air and left, leaving me staring stupidly at a blank door with whatever I might have said in reply still lost in a half-drawn breath.

CHAPTER THIRTEEN

"**C**harmer," someone said behind me.

"Yeah," I agreed, turning slowly. "One of your all-time sweethearts."

Parker was standing behind me, coffee cup in hand. Cisco wagged his tail even harder and moved toward him. I stopped him with a firm hand-command to sit. Cisco obeyed, his tail still swishing along the floor, happy eyes still watching Parker in expectation of something good coming his way.

Parker looked down at Cisco, eyes crinkling with a smile. "Is it okay if I pet him? Or..." he gestured to the leash in my hand. "Is he being punished for earlier misbehavior?"

I was embarrassed. "Sorry about your socks," I said. "He's a little excitable. And you can pet him, as long as he stays sitting."

Parker knelt down and gave Cisco's ears a hearty

rub, finishing with a scratch under the chin. Cisco lapped it up. "My kids would love a dog like this," he said, standing. "All they're allowed to have now is a little Peek-a-Something that doesn't do anything but yap and lift its leg on the furniture. They don't even know what a real dog is. They live in Chicago with my ex-wife," he explained. "The building doesn't allow dogs over twenty pounds."

I smiled sympathetically but kept my opinion to myself. That opinion being, basically, that there are no bad dogs, just bad owners.

He said, "I wanted to apologize for coming on to you earlier. It was inappropriate."

I shrugged it away, my cheeks pinkening. "Then we're even." I gestured awkwardly to Cisco. "His behavior was inappropriate too."

Parker took a sip of his coffee. "So how long have you and Miles known each other?"

"A couple of years. He bought the property next to mine and built his house there."

"Right." Parker nodded thoughtfully, seeming to put the picture together. "He's living in North Carolina now. In the mountains. I keep meaning to get down that way but I'm in the New York office now and there's not a lot of free time."

I said a little awkwardly, "Miles spends a lot of time going back and forth to Atlanta."

He seemed to cast about for something else to say and settled on Cisco. "So, what's the deal with not feeding your dog? Allergies or something?"

"Cisco is a working dog," I explained. "Food is

his paycheck. If you started getting paid for doing nothing, how long would you work?"

He chuckled. "Good point." He grinned at Cisco and said, "You and me, Cisco, brothers under the skin." Then he looked at me. "Do you think he could really get you out of the woods if you were lost?"

"He's trained in wilderness search and rescue," I said. "If I were lost, he would find me. Lacking a specific target, he will move toward the closest sign of human activity—that could be a road, or a house, or a campsite. And if I follow him, I'll eventually find safety. But," I added quickly, "that's not the smartest thing to do. It's always best to remain where you are and let rescue come to you."

He nodded. "Under normal circumstances."

"Right," I agreed. "Which I guess we're not talking about here."

In the kitchen, BJ laughed at something Miles said, and when I looked their way, Miles was laughing too.

I turned back to Parker. "I get the feeling you've taken this survival course before."

He lifted a modest shoulder. "Something like it. In the military, a couple of thousand years ago. Never had to use any of it, thank God."

I said uncertainly, "So... seriously. The company doesn't really send people to places where there are terrorists and hostage-takers and stuff like that, right? I mean, why would it? You just build hotels, don't you?"

He smiled. "For the most part, yes. But like the man said, things happen. Planes go down, unstable governments collapse, wars break out, sometimes overnight." He shrugged. "It doesn't hurt to be prepared."

I frowned a little. "Miles said something about a man last year. Brett? What happened to him?"

Parker turned his gaze to his coffee cup, a line appearing between his brows. "That," he said quietly, "was bad. Everyone was upset, naturally, but Miles most of all. Brett was scouting sites for a new factory in Venezuela when he was taken captive by one of the warlords and held for ransom. We were ready to pay it, of course, and Miles wanted to lead the rescue mission himself. But it didn't matter. We got word within days that Brett was already dead."

I felt a coldness in my stomach, a knot in my throat. This time last year we'd been drinking hot chocolate and arguing about where to spend Thanksgiving. Miles had never said a word about any of this. The gap between Miles's world and mine became a chasm.

Before I could say anything, or even think of anything to say, Reed Barnes's booming voice interrupted. I was glad.

"Sandoval, let me bring you up to date on the Naples project while we have the chance." Reed already had his hand on Parker's arm. "You don't mind if I borrow him for a minute, do you, um, Remy?"

"Raine," I corrected absently.

He waved a congenial hand. "Right. Rae, Riley, River, I knew it was something like that. So, here's the situation," he turned to Parker, giving me his back.

Parker shot me an apologetic look and I murmured, "I think I'll go feed Cisco."

But Reed was already well into his point about whatever it was he had wanted to talk to Parker about, and I left without receiving a reply.

It should be obvious by now that Cisco, for all his accomplishments, is not known for his laid-back temperament. If there is trouble to get into, he will find it, which is why keeping an eye on him is more or less a full-time job. I had traveled with Cisco a lot, and I thought I had the routine down pat. But the places we went were usually, by definition, dog-friendly: dog shows, conferences, workshops, training camps. These places were not only designed to accommodate dogs, but everyone there *had* a dog—some of them worse-behaved than Cisco. I was beginning to worry I had underestimated the challenges of spending a week at a non-dog event among non-dog people with my very talented, extremely demanding dog.

After what had happened earlier, I certainly was not comfortable leaving him alone in the bunk room with everyone else's possessions, and some people might object to having a dog at the table while we ate. So after Cisco finished his dinner and I took him for a short walk around the lodge, I spread his sleeping mat on the floor of the small radio room and left him with his water bowl and a bone to chew. Aside from a filing cabinet and the radio equipment on a tall table, there was nothing in there but a set of steel shelves with some sealed boxes toward the top and I didn't think

Cisco would be able to do any harm while I was gone. He gave me a mildly reproachful look when I gave him the command to "wait," but he was already stretched out on his mat chewing his bone when I closed the door behind me.

I heard Miles say, "All right, folks, come and get it. And keep in mind, we didn't cook it, we just heated it up."

Chairs scraped and voices chattered with at least three different conversations as I came into the room. "I left Cisco in the radio room," I said. "Does anyone mind?"

No one replied or even glanced around. I took that to mean no one minded. Either that, or I was fast becoming the Invisible Woman.

We all found places at the table while Miles and BJ brought aluminum casserole dishes, salad, and bottles of dressing. Someone made a remark about the instant sweet tea in their glasses and Miles replied, "A proud Southern tradition since 1962"—which I didn't appreciate. Everyone in the South knows it takes at least half a day to make good sweet tea.

When everyone was settled, Miles took his place across from me and glanced around. "Where's Steele?"

Theo replied, "Probably in town dining on tomahawk steaks and truffled potatoes. I saw him roaring out of here in a big-ass Lincoln Navigator about half an hour ago."

Max was outraged. "He has a *car*? I thought the only way to get here was to hike in."

While Miles explained about the service access

road, BJ—who, I couldn't help noticing, had chosen a seat next to him—passed around the casserole. There were some jokes about the food; the overweight Reed Barnes declaring, "What? No vegan options? Oh, dear, oh, dear, whatever shall I do?" In answer, BJ shoved the salad bowl in front of him, which he passed down the line, taking an extra helping of the casserole.

BJ said, "Miles, do you remember that horrible dinner we had in Bogota? What was it, again? Fox?"

"Monkey," replied Miles, and everyone took a second look at the casserole on their plates.

"When in Rome," said Parker, and gamely took a bite.

In fact, the casserole wasn't that different from what might have been on my table on any random Tuesday when Miles was out of town. Cheese, pasta, ground beef, tomato sauce—what's not to like? I tried not to dwell on the differences between the others at the table and myself, but it became even more difficult when, tired of mocking the food, the conversations turned to business. Words like "fourth-quarter returns" and "straight-line acquisitions" droned in my head, and I did not even pretend to be interested.

At one point Theo, obviously trying to find a way to make nice with the boss's girl, asked me, "Where did you go to school, Raine?"

"North Carolina," I replied, and he brightened.

"Really? Me, too."

"I meant state," I explained.

His expression fell. "I meant Duke."

"Of course you did," I murmured and turned back

to my meal. He looked relieved not to have to try to make conversation with a woman who'd attended a state college.

I don't attend many corporate functions with Miles, mostly because he doesn't attend many corporate functions, and I never felt as though I was missing anything. Once Miles gave an open house that was attended by senators and billionaires and media celebrities whose names I probably should have known, but I spent most of my time hanging out with Melanie. On occasion, people from his company visited him at home, and he introduced me to them, but I never remembered their names. For the first time, I wondered if this was a failing on my part. For the first time, I think I actually began to understand how very alien this part of Miles's life was to me, and how much I didn't belong.

As the mostly unintelligible conversations went on around me, Ian, making one more attempt to engage me, murmured, "Is this all as fascinating to you as it is to me?"

I gave a surprised grunt of laughter, relieved to hear that someone was as baffled as I was. "What? I thought all this talk of annuities and prospectuses would be right up your alley, being that you insure it all."

He shook his head, smiling. "I'm more of a numbers man. This is so far over my head I'd fall asleep if I weren't so hungry."

"I'm glad I'm not the only one," I admitted.

He said, "So, how did you become a wilderness

guide?"

"Oh." I was a little taken aback. "Um, that's not officially what I do. I mean, I don't lead expeditions for a living or anything. I hope that doesn't disqualify me."

He looked blank. "From what?"

"Miles said the insurance company required two certified wilderness experts to teach the course," I said. "I thought that was why you were here—to make sure."

"Right," he said and smiled. He added, "To be honest, we're not all that strict about the particulars. Could you pass the bread, please?"

I started to ask why, if that was the case, it had seemed so important to Miles that I be here, but at that moment Max, who was sitting on Ian's other side, asked him something about annuities and he turned his attention to her. I passed the bread and tuned the conversation out.

Miles, for his part, had spent the dinner doing what he does best: listening. Since knowing him, I'd developed a theory: listening is how smart men get smarter and rich men get richer. As we finished our meal, he spoke up.

"I hope you all have got that out of your systems," he said, "because from now on, there's a rule—no business talk. That's what e-mail is for."

Immediately, everyone fell silent. The silence went on for so long that it was clear they had no idea what to talk about once the only thing they had in common was taken off the table.

Miles's mouth quirked with amusement as he suggested, "Family? Children? Football? The fastest route to Chicago?"

BJ chuckled as she stood. "Oh, please. You should know these people have no life outside the office. How about this?" She placed her hands briefly on Miles's shoulders as she passed behind his chair. "I saw some hot chocolate mix in one of the cabinets. You boys go build a fire in that firepit outside and I'll heat up some water in the coffee urn. We can have a nice old-fashioned campfire cocoa and chat before bed."

Everyone agreed, with perhaps more enthusiasm than could be considered genuine, that that sounded fine. I started gathering up the dishes, figuring that was the least could do after Miles and BJ cooked. I expected someone to offer to help, but no one did.

Max said, "Well, I'm going to take a shower even if it isn't between the hours of 5:30 and 6:00 a.m. And if anyone tries to stop me, you should know I have pepper spray and I'm not afraid to use it."

Reed started searching the cabinets for the ingredients for s'mores while Miles and Ian went outside to get the fire started. Everyone else filled their mugs with packaged hot chocolate mix and joked about how long it had been since they'd had it. For me, it was last weekend. Water gurgled in the urn as it heated, and by the time I finished clearing the table, everyone had taken their instant hot chocolate and was moving outdoors. I filled the sink with soapy water and finished the dishes by myself. For the first time that day, I actually felt useful.

Needless to say, I wasn't particularly interested in joining the others by the campfire. I put away the last of the dishes and pulled on my jacket with the intention of taking Cisco for one last walk and turning in early. It might be the last chance I had to get Cisco settled down before everyone else came trooping back into the bunk room and got him too excited to sleep. I added another one of the complications of bringing Cisco along on this trip to the ones I hadn't thought of: communal sleeping.

"Come on, bud," I said, opening the radio room door. "Let's go for a walk."

The scrabbling nails and wagging tail I expected did not greet me. Instead, the room was heavy with silence.

Cisco wasn't there.

CHAPTER FOURTEEN

Most people did not realize how expansive the forest really was, how many coves and valleys and cliffs and hiding places existed within it. By the time dusk arrived, Jessup felt as though he had covered most of that expanse and was intimately familiar with its secrets. That was a fallacy, he knew, and he would never be so arrogant as to convince himself of it. But he was entirely confident that he had done as much as any man could do to secure his continued survival in this particular forest.

His most immediate problem was the unexpected interference of the park ranger. Tomorrow, or perhaps the next day, they would send up drones or even helicopters to look for her. They wouldn't find her, at least not all at once. He spent hours with a hacksaw to make certain of that. Her jeep, of course, was a second problem. He drove it as far into the forest as he could, deep into seldom-traversed park service land, and buried it in a mound of evergreen so thick even drones would not be able to distinguish it from the surrounding terrain.

He drove miles disposing of the body parts, and when he returned to the trail that led to the lodge, he realized he had used most of the gas in the pickup. He had almost abandoned his initial idea of re-provisioning at the lodge, but now he had no choice. There was gasoline in the storage shed there. There were also, according to the park ranger, people.

He hid the truck in the deep woods far off the service road and hiked across country to the lodge, avoiding the trails. This was no hardship for him, even after a day of such physical exertion as he had had. He was accustomed to hiking ten or twenty miles a day in all kinds of weather, hunting for and cleaning his kill, then chopping wood for fire and shelter at night. That was the life he had chosen, the one he was good at.

It was full dark when he settled on the ridge overlooking the lodge. Lamplight glowed faintly through the windows, and someone had built a fire outdoors. He settled on his belly and took out his binoculars. He counted three—no, four—people around the fire. A woman coming from the showers. Another man crossed the yard toward the house. Six of them. Now another woman. So at least seven. There was a vehicle inside the car shed, which could mean any number of people inside. He could of course lie in wait and pick them off from here, one by one, but that would be stupid and wasteful. Also unnecessarily risky. He had not stayed alive this long by indulging in stupidity, waste, or unnecessary risk. There was a better way. Patience was the key.

Jessup stilled at the sound of a rustling in the brush below him. Slowly, silently, he reached over his shoulder, took up the crossbow, found an arrow in the quiver, and loaded it. He turned so smoothly, so silently toward the approaching sound that even a laser-equipped night scope could not have detected his movement. In the darkness, he saw a pair of phosphorescent yellow eyes. He settled his finger on the trigger of the crossbow.

With a low whine, the dog crept out of the undergrowth. It was a golden retriever, possibly the most harmless creature on the face of the earth. Jessup removed his finger from the trigger and lowered the weapon. He said softly, "Hey there, buddy." The dog, swishing its tail lowly, crept closer. Jessup stroked one silky ear. "You lost?"

Dogs could be a problem for a man like him. They could find things in the woods humans never would. They would bark alarms long before humans heard the sound. But Jessup had a code, and disposing of a harmless animal simply because it might be a threat was not only unethical, it was wasteful.

He presumed the dog belonged to someone at the lodge, and in a moment, he was proven right. He heard the woman calling and saw the dog's ears prick in response. The one thing he didn't want was people combing the woods, looking for a lost dog. He had some venison jerky in his pocket and let the dog sniff it. The animal's demeanor perked up considerably and he followed Jessup happily as he led him through the woods, closer to the lodge. When he was a couple of hundred yards away, he threw the piece of meat toward the lodge. The dog scampered after it and Jessup slipped away, disappearing into the forest while the dog was still sniffing for the jerky.

His surveillance was complete, and Jessup had work to do.

CHAPTER FIFTEEN

I moved quickly across the hall to the bunk room, calling, "Cisco! Cisco, here!" The bunk room was empty, sleeping bags open atop cots, packs resting on footlockers or bunks in varying states of disarray, the glass doors of the woodstove sending a red glow across the floor. Logically, I knew Cisco would come if he could hear my voice, and I could plainly see he wasn't there, but where else could he be? I felt compelled to turn on every lamp, to look under every cot. Nothing.

There was a door at the end of the corridor, the shortest route to the bathrooms and showers. Maybe he had accidentally gotten out when Max went to take her shower. I grabbed my flashlight from my pack and started toward it as the door across from the bunk room opened.

"Lose your dog?" Steele said.

"He was in the radio room," I said, trying not to sound as panicked as I was beginning to feel. "Did you see him? Did you let him out?"

Steele just shook his head in disgust and closed the door.

I opened the back door and called Cisco's name. A flashlight beam was coming toward me, and I stepped outside, recognizing Max, bundled up in a jacket and sweats with her hair wrapped in a skimpy towel.

"Now that," she declared unhappily, shivering, "was a totally miserable experience. I don't recommend it."

"Have you seen Cisco?" I demanded.

She looked puzzled. "Who?"

"My dog. Was he out there? Did he get out when you opened the door?"

She shrugged. "I didn't see him."

I pushed past her into the dark, sweeping my flashlight beam in front of me. "Cisco! Cisco, here!"

The night was cold and damp and scented with woodsmoke. My quick, puffing breath frosted before me. "Cisco!" I called again.

My light picked up the fingerbone shapes of low bushes and the rounded shadows of dark woods, but nothing else. How long had he been gone? How far might he have gotten? These woods were unfamiliar to him; he did not know that this was where he belonged or that he should make his way back here if he was separated from me. He might just as easily try to retrace his steps on the trail up here or start across country toward the nearest house, which could be miles away. How many lost dogs did we pick up every year whose vacationing owners had stupidly thought they could let their dogs out "just for a minute," assuming that they would stay close to the cabin or campsite because they never left the yard at home? Sometimes we were able to reunite the dogs with their owners, but for the most part, by the time someone turned them into the shelter or to breed rescue, it was too late.

I could hear voices coming from the front of the building where the firepit was, and I moved toward them, telling myself that I was panicking over nothing. Of course that's where Cisco was. Even if he had slipped through an accidentally opened door, he would immediately go to where the people were. He was probably in the center of the activity right now, mooching pats and basking in the attention. Or maybe Miles had taken him out without telling me. It wasn't the kind of thing he usually did, but who knew?

I almost bumped into Parker as I came around the side of the building. He didn't have a flashlight, so I saw him before he saw me, and he gave a startled laugh when he was able to identify my face. "Hey," he said. "I'm glad you decided to join us. Where's your dog?"

My heart sank. "You haven't seen him? He's not at the campfire?"

I could see his expression grow concerned in the reflected beam of my flashlight. "Not that I saw," he said. "Is he missing?"

I moved past him without answering, calling for Cisco.

They had a good-sized bonfire going and BJ,

Theo, and Reed were sitting on the circular bench surrounding it, sipping from mugs and chuckling over some joke Reed had made. Cisco was nowhere to be seen.

Miles and Ian each dumped an armload of wood inside the circle and Miles said, "I need volunteers to stock the dorm room and the keeping room with firewood for the night. I volunteer Theo and Parker. Where is Parker, anyway?"

"I sent him inside for cookies," BJ said. "You know those iced gingersnaps you like?"

Miles glanced around and saw me. "Hey, babe. Where's Cisco?"

I said in a fast, tight voice, "Did any of you let Cisco out? He was in the radio room." I looked urgently from one to the other of them. "Have you seen him?"

I was met with blank, confused stares. Reed said, "You mean your dog?"

Theo said, "Where's the radio room?"

And all BJ had to offer was, "Did you lose him?"

Miles took his flashlight from his pocket and touched my arm lightly. "You go east, I'll go west."

BJ stood. "We can help you look."

Reed and Theo were less enthusiastic, but they stood as well. "Sure," one of them said. "What's his name again?" Miles was, after all, their boss, and I was the boss's girlfriend and Cisco was my dog. They wanted to appear helpful, and their help was the last thing I needed.

I held up a quick staying hand. "No. Too many flashlights and voices will just confuse him. We'll find him."

BJ said, "Are you sure? I don't mind."

Ian added, "I'd like to help. Hate to think of anything happening to the little fellow, so far from home."

I had already turned toward the wood line to start my search, so Miles said to both of them, "Raine's right. The fewer people searching, the better. But thanks."

We walked away from the fire, and I spoke rapidly, trying to think it through. "He must have gotten out the back door. Someone would have seen him otherwise. That means he's probably in the woods somewhere. Dogs travel in scent circles so we should start close to the building and arc out into the woods. I don't know how long he's been gone so there's no way of telling how far into the woods he got. We'll make one pass about twenty feet out and then meet up and cross our paths."

"We should stop by the kitchen and get some food," Miles said.

I was ashamed I hadn't thought of that sooner. That's what dry-mouthed fear would do. And if I was this scared, how must Cisco feel all alone in a strange forest and nothing to show him the way home?

I said, "Good idea. Something smelly, like tuna or canned salmon. And maybe potato chips. You know how he is with the sound of that bag."

Miles slipped his arm around my shoulders in a quick, reassuring hug. "We've got this, sugar. Cisco's a smart dog and he's not going to leave you. Don't panic, okay?"

"Yeah." I breathed out, breathed in, and tried not to think about the times Cisco had left me before —on the trail of a deer, racing to greet a random stranger, leaping into the lap of someone he knew. He was a golden retriever. Smart, loyal, loveable, and completely unpredictable. "Okay," I managed in a moment. "Right. Okay."

We had reached the steps of the lodge when someone called to us from the dark, "Looking for this?"

I turned toward the sound of the voice and was briefly blinded by the glare of a flashlight coming toward us from about fifty feet away. As I flung up my arm to shield my eyes, Parker lowered his light and I saw he was holding something in his other hand. It was a leash, and at the end of the leash trotted Cisco.

I dropped to my knees on a single muffled gasp, opening my arms. Cisco leapt forward, ripping the leash from Parker's hand, and ran toward me, knocking me flat on my butt with his exuberance. I wrapped my arms around his neck and buried my face in his fur, exclaiming nonsensically, "Good dog, good dog, what a good dog! Where've you been, huh? What happened to you? Oh, what a good dog!"

When Parker drew closer, Miles said, "Where'd you find him?"

Parker gestured over his shoulder. "Back there at the edge of the woods. I thought I saw his eyes glinting in the dark, but when I turned my beam on him, he started to run away. I got him back with this."

Something crinkled in his hand, and Cisco's ears pricked. When I glanced up Parker held up a cellophane bag of cookies and gave me an apologetic smile. "Sorry I broke your rule," he said, "but the only way I could get him to come to me was with a cookie. I thought maybe it would be okay just this once."

"Yeah." I breathed out a shaky breath and stood, twining Cisco's leash tightly between my fingers. "Just this once."

"He doesn't look too much the worse for wear," Parker added. "I don't think he wandered too far away."

Cisco's fur was damp with evening dew and tangled with a few dried leaves and twigs. His leash was muddy and knotted, but from his grin and madly wagging tail, I had to agree that he was none the worse for wear. "Thanks, Parker," I said. My voice was still a little unsteady. "Really."

"No problem. Glad I spotted him."

Miles clapped him on the shoulder. "Come on, let's see if you and Cisco left any of those cookies for the rest of us. Raine, I kept your chocolate warm by the fire."

But I was still too unsteady to be around the others just yet. I said, "I'll be right there. I just want to give Cisco some water and dry him off."

I gave Cisco's leash a gentle tug and started toward the steps. Then I stopped. His leash. I turned to look at Parker. "Where'd you find his leash?" I asked.

Parker and Miles had started back toward the firepit, and Parker's expression was confused as he looked back at me. "I didn't," he said. "He was wearing it."

I gave him another quick smile of thanks and went up the stairs into the lodge, Cisco trotting happily at my side. But my heart was pounding, and no longer from relief. I *never* left Cisco unattended with his leash on. He could choke or get tangled up or—even more likely—chew through the expensive fabric out of boredom. I distinctly remembered folding it and leaving it atop the radio table when I left him with his bone in the radio room. Someone had put the leash on Cisco and deliberately led him into the woods, then left him there.

My breath came in harsh drags as I marched down the dimly lit corridor to the bunk room. I paused to pound on the closed door across from it with my fist, calling out to Steele, "I found my dog!" and I muttered under my breath, "You son of a bitch."

He didn't even bother to open the door.

CHAPTER SIXTEEN

I took my time brushing the burrs and tangles out of Cisco's fur, soothing myself—and him—with the motion. Everyone knows that your emotions go straight down the leash to your dog, so if you spend much time around dogs, you condition yourself to stay calm in a crisis, to keep your voice low when you feel like screaming and your steps slow when you want to run. Of course, I was still furious and deeply shaken, and it was all I could do to keep my imagination from racing down that scary "what if" path. But to Cisco, I was his safe place. It was important that I remain so.

Cisco stretched out on his towel in front of the woodstove in the main room and I brushed him until his eyes were mere slits of contentment and his coat was as shiny as the golden glow of the fire. One by one the others drifted in, put their mugs in the sink (didn't *any* of them know how to wash a dish?), and said good night. Some of them made a casual comment about being glad I had found my dog. Cisco thumped his tail to each and every one.

Finally, I put away the brush and towel, put on my jacket, and took up Cisco's leash for one last walk before turning in. He yawned, stretched, and shook a halo of golden fur into the air before trotting to the door. Cisco was excellent at not holding a grudge. Regrettably, that's one thing we will never have in common.

Miles finished smothering the campfire with sand from a pile beside the firepit and met me halfway across the yard. His flashlight beam joined with mine, and we moved slowly around the perimeter, following Cisco as he paused to sniff and pee on every bush. Occasionally his ears pricked up at the sound of something scurrying through the dead leaves, and I tightened my hand on his leash. The night was dark and heavy around us, the stars obscured by cloud cover and the faint glow of lamplight from the lodge swallowed up by the depth of shadows. It's impossible to appreciate how dark night can be until you get away from the ambient light of civilization. It's something few people get a chance to experience.

I said, "Why didn't you tell anyone we were engaged?"

"I told people," he objected. "My mom, Mel…"

"These people," I interrupted. "Your colleagues. Your top executives. People you know, and like."

He replied, "I'm not sure. It might have something

to do with the fact that it took you six weeks to give me an answer, six months to set a date, and you've postponed that date three times so far. Maybe I'm a little insecure."

I responded a little stiffly, "It wasn't always my fault. A couple of times you were the one who had to change the date."

"We have complicated schedules," he agreed mildly, which I suppose was meant to remind me that he was the only one who even had a schedule.

After a time I said, "I talked to Ian, that insurance guy, at dinner, and he didn't seem to think having two instructors here was all that much of a big deal. In fact, he didn't even seem to know it was a rule. So, I was thinking. I could give my third-grade lecture on wildlife safety, or whatever it is you need me to do for insurance purposes, first thing in the morning. It won't take me much more than an hour to hike back down to the road, and I can call Casey from there. He could pick me up by noon, and I'll be home before supper."

Our footsteps crunched on the frosty dried grass, and Cisco stopped to examine something at the edge of the woods. I urged him away with a light snap of the leash. You never can tell what a golden retriever is going to put in his mouth.

Miles said, "Is this because of what happened with Cisco?"

I didn't try to pretend otherwise. "I think Steele let him out."

I could feel him nod his head thoughtfully. "Maybe.

Makes sense. Max said she saw his car behind the building when she went to shower. Plenty of time for him to take Cisco while we were out here fooling with the fire."

That was all he had to say? *Makes sense?* No outrage on my behalf, no defense of Cisco? Once again, that didn't sound at all like Miles.

I said, "Steele doesn't want me here, and, like I said, Ian from the insurance company didn't seem to think it made much difference whether I was here or not. Steele is not going to let me do my job—if there ever even was a job."

"What's that supposed to mean?"

I sighed heavily. "Come on, Miles, the only reason I'm here is because you felt sorry for me. You were trying to distract me like you'd try to cheer up Melanie when she's pouting by buying her a pony."

He objected, "I never bought her a pony."

I ignored him. "Well, I'm not ten years old and I don't want your pity. I just want to go home."

He said, "You don't need me to feel sorry for you. You're doing too good a job of that all by yourself."

I looked at him sharply. "That's not fair."

"Look," he said. There was a touch of impatience in his voice. "I know you've had a rough year. I was there, remember? You took some hits, you lost a lot. But Raine, that's not why your life is on the skids. You're the one who closed down your business for six weeks, and when you did open back up you didn't even send out an e-blast to let people know. You only taught one class a week and pretty soon you stopped that."

"It wasn't worth it," I protested. "There were only three people in the last class! That didn't even pay the light bill."

"You stopped going to dog shows, you stopped posting on social media," he went on. "Your clients probably thought you were dead. You dropped out of pretty much every organization you were involved with. You stopped answering the phone. You barely even left the house. You've got no one to blame but yourself for what's happened to you, and you know it. So no, I don't feel sorry for you. Not by a long shot. But damn it, Raine, you've never run away from a fight in your life and I can't believe you're going to let a fourth-class bully like Steele force you into doing it now."

I had absolutely no argument to offer. He was right. I knew he was right and hearing him say it out loud made me angry and ashamed. But it did not make me want to stay.

I said quietly, "It's not just Steele. I don't belong here, Miles. These people... they're all nice enough, but we live in completely different worlds. None of them think I'm good enough for you..."

"They don't think that," he interrupted. There was a touch of dismissive impatience in his voice.

"Well, they make me think that," I said. I kept my eyes on the end of the leash, and the golden retriever shape illuminated by the beam of my flashlight, mostly because I did not want Miles to see my face, even in the dark. "They remind me that there's this whole part of your life—maybe the biggest part— that I don't know, and that I wouldn't understand if

I did. God, Miles, you didn't even bother to mention to me that one of your employees was kidnapped and murdered by a warlord, and you were ready to risk your life to save him!   Is that the kind of thing that happens so often that you don't think it's worth bringing up in conversation? Or did you think I wouldn't be interested? And now you've got this whole spy thing going on right here under my nose and you won't even tell me the details. It's just…" I shook my head and drew in a long, deep breath. "I mean I've always known it, but I've just started to really see how very different our lives are, and… I need some time, okay?"

We had reached the firepit, and Miles touched my shoulder lightly. "Let's sit for a minute."

I shook my head. I didn't want to have this conversation now. I was afraid of where it might lead. "Miles, it's cold, and I'm tired. Let's…"

But he insisted firmly, "It's important."

Reluctantly, I let him lead me to the stone bench, where there was some residual warmth from the fire, and we sat down, turning off our flashlights. I said, "Is this another stupid fish story?"

"Not exactly."

I drew Cisco's head onto my knee, stroking his ears. After a moment Miles spoke.

"When I moved to Hanover County," he said, "built my house there, and decided to raise Melanie there, it was because I was looking for a sanctuary. I told you that. Some place as far away from my daily life, my responsibilities and concerns, as I could get. There are always going to be things I don't tell you about my work, Raine. Not because I don't want you to know, or because I don't think you'd be interested—although most of the time, I'm pretty sure you wouldn't be..." I could sense his smile in the dark. "But because I need one place in my life that's clean and pure and easy, completely disconnected from all that I have to deal with on a daily basis. You, and Mom and Melanie— you're that place. That safe place. Can you understand that?"

I nodded slowly, feeling bad now for being impatient with him. "Yeah," I said quietly. "I understand. I mean, okay, I get it when you can't tell me why you really went to Belgium or why you have the Assistant Director of Homeland Security's personal cell phone number, or how you can order a whole fleet of helicopters into an evacuation zone when law enforcement can't... Those are the parts of being rich and powerful that I'm better off not knowing. And I don't mind. Really. In fact, I think it's kind of hot."

He threaded his fingers through mine, warming them.

"But," I went on carefully, "understanding doesn't change anything. In fact, it makes it worse, in a way. I'm up here in the middle of nowhere and I don't even know why, my so-called boss hates me, somebody tried to steal my dog, and I've got a right to know what's going on. So either tell me, or I'm leaving. That's"—I sucked in a breath and exhaled it sharply —"all I've got to say."

Miles was silent for so long that I thought he'd taken me up on my offer after all, and I would be leaving in the morning. But he did not let go of my hand. And finally, he said, "You know what I said earlier, about the most important survival tool being a partner you can trust? I didn't just say that to get on your good side. I needed you here for a reason, and I might have manipulated a few things to get you here. I apologize for that."

I probably should have been offended by that, but in fact, I was intrigued. Now, at last, maybe we'd get to the truth. I said, "Such as?"

He said, "I paid Steele's assistant not to come so that I could put you in his place, and the insurance requirement that we have two instructors on site was more of a suggestion than a requirement. I'm sorry. It was the best I could come up with on short notice. And..." He sighed and pushed a hand through his short-cropped hair. "I guess you already figured out there's no place for a tracking dog demo in the curriculum."

My lips turned down dryly. "Right. Got that."

"The reason I didn't give you any details about what was going on," he continued, "was because I hoped I wouldn't have to. That I was wrong. That none of these people were involved. That we'd have a couple of days hiking and camping, and we'd laugh about this in the car on the way home."

He fell silent, and I prompted, "But?"

Miles took out his phone and thumbed through a couple of screens before turning it toward me. All I could see was what looked like, at first glance, a very bad satellite photo of a forest. A small red dot blinked in the center of it. Miles enlarged the photo and I saw what might have been the roof of this very lodge. The red dot continued to blink in the center.

"It's a tracking signal, of sorts," he explained. "Yesterday, someone downloaded the source code for a top-secret piece of software we've spent the last five years developing. It hardens smart-homes and—more importantly—smart buildings against cyberattacks. It's worth billions. This signal was embedded into the code. It bounces off a satellite and goes directly to my phone, showing me where the drive containing the stolen software is located."

"So..." I squinted through the dark at the glowing image on his phone, as though studying it would somehow make the whole thing clearer for me. "What you're looking for is here? At the lodge?"

He nodded and put the phone away. "Which means that one of these people, one of my most trusted executives, is the thief."

All I could think to say was, "I'm sorry." Then I added uncertainly, "So who is it?"

He shook his head. "I don't know yet. The signal is only accurate within a hundred yards. My guess is that he—or she—plans to pass the storage device on to a buyer, or leave it to be collected later, somewhere here in the wilderness. It's not a bad idea when you think about it. This might be the one place on earth where there are no security cameras, no listening devices, no way to detect movement. And the thief has a perfect excuse for being here—a corporate-sanctioned event."

"So you have to wait until he tries to pass it off to find out who it is," I said.

"More or less."

"Miles," I said hesitantly, "that doesn't sound like such a great plan."

He laughed softly in the dark, shaking his head. "It's the only one I've got. And," he added, "maybe not quite as foolish as it sounds. Aside from the fact that I have an expert private security team monitoring the thief's every move with the same tracking signal that's on my phone, what he stole wasn't actually of any value at all. The code he downloaded has a concealed flaw that makes it inoperable. So even if he gets away with it, he won't get away with it. I just..." His tone hardened fractionally. "Need to know who it is."

I slipped my arm through his and leaned my head against his shoulder. Cisco added his own measure of comfort by placing both front paws on Miles's knees. Miles put one arm around me and stroked Cisco's head with his other hand.

"You know," I said thoughtfully, "there are probably going to be times when everybody is out of the lodge. Plenty of opportunity to search backpacks."

"Now, you see? That's just the kind of borderline-illegal thinking I need you along for. But if it were me, I wouldn't leave something that valuable in a backpack. I'd keep it on me at all times."

I thought some more. "Then we need to find a way to separate the thief and his stolen software from everyone else. Then it would show up on your phone, right?"

"Right," he agreed.

We sat for a while longer, plotting softly in the dark, brainstorming ideas to isolate and identify the person with the tracking signal embedded into the top-secret code—a code that was not top secret after all and that was, in fact, worthless—in order to catch the thief who had stolen nothing.

How very foolish we mice must have looked to the raptor who watched us so steadily, so stealthily, from his perch on the ridge high above.

CHAPTER SEVENTEEN

The night passed about as well as could be expected considering the circumstances. The circumstances being a bunch of pampered city-types whose last experience with "roughing it" had probably been a prep school summer camp.

Max and BJ had set up a privacy corner by stretching a sheet or curtain—heaven knew where they'd found it—from one corner to another so they could change into their pajamas. Max, at least, wore practical flannels, but BJ wore navy silk with white piping that was immediately covered in yellow dog hair. That's the thing about golden retrievers. All you have to do is walk through a room to get covered in hair; actually touching the dog is not a requirement.

I tried to point out, as tactfully as possible, that most people slept in their sweats or their underwear on camping trips. The two women, smelling of outrageously expensive beauty creams and body wash, looked at me as though I'd suggested they serve red wine with fish for dinner.

Of course, cordoning off a corner of the room meant pushing the cots closer together. Reed made some lame joke about sleeping with the boss, which wasn't all that funny considering BJ's former relationship with Miles. Worse, Cisco took the rearranging of the sleeping space as an invitation to bounce from cot to cot greeting everyone—a notion I was fortunately able to discourage as soon as it got started. But that did point out another problem of having Cisco along. In a dog camp or workshop situation there was usually a crating room where all the dogs spent the night, or, barring that, arrangements were made for the dogs to stay in the room with their owners. Cisco does not crate well, and I hadn't really considered how I was going to keep him from wandering around a room full of strangers all night. Eventually, Miles and I solved the problem by turning one cot on its side between our two beds, virtually boxing Cisco in. I could tell that traveling with a dog under these circumstances was going to be nothing but one problem after another. And even though I felt disloyal for saying it, I couldn't help muttering to Miles, "Tell me again why we wanted to bring Cisco along?"

He replied with a raised eyebrow, "Because he's part of the team. Right?"

Okay. Points for Miles.

The next day dawned cold and gray, and when I checked my hiking watch for the regional forecast, I saw rain was expected to move in the following afternoon. That meant, unless Steele was a complete sadist, today would be our last opportunity for outdoor exercises for a while. And that meant today would also be our best chance to separate the members of the group and isolate the tracking signal.

Although, with Steele in charge of the activities, I didn't see how we were going to manage that.

Breakfast was a half-hearted attempt at individual bowls of cereal or toaster pastries with lots of grimaces over the canned milk and complaints about the rough night's sleep. This time, Cisco's leash remained firmly clipped to the D-ring on my hiking pants, and if anyone objected to a dog in the kitchen they didn't say anything to me. To his credit, Cisco was exceptionally well behaved, walking right at my knee, sitting when I stopped, and keeping the floor-sniffing and crumb-scarfing to a minimum. Of course, that all fell apart as soon as someone held out a hand to him or greeted him in one of those baby-voices people like to use with dogs. Cisco might be an exceptional canine, but he was, after all, a canine.

I finished my instant oatmeal quickly and took Cisco out for his after-breakfast walk. When I returned, Steele had moved the whiteboard in front of the woodstove in the main lounge and was replacing yesterday's "S.T.O.P." mnemonic with the three survival priorities: food, water, and shelter. They were in the wrong order, I couldn't help noticing.

I walked up to him and said, "Rain is forecast for tomorrow. I had planned some outdoor woodcraft demos—you know, what plants are safe to eat, how to avoid dangerous wildlife, that kind of thing—and today would be a good day to do that." I kept a hand on Cisco's leash, close to the collar, just in case he decided to try to make friends with Steele. Cisco, though, was much more interested in Parker, who had brought a cinnamon roll on a paper plate into the room along with his coffee.

"Is that right?" Without turning from the board, Steele raised his voice. "All right, people, get your coffee and find a seat."

My lips compressed in annoyance. "You know, Mr. Steele, I am not here for you to ignore. Both Mr. Young and the insurance company asked for my expertise, and I intend to give it with or without your permission. You are not," I added pointedly, "irreplaceable." Now that I knew what was really at stake, I had no problem playing the diva. In fact, I rather enjoyed it. I enjoyed it so much that I couldn't help adding, "And you've got your priorities out of order." I pointed at the board.

He turned to look at me just as Miles walked up. "All set for today?" Miles inquired pleasantly, although it was obvious he had heard us arguing.

I replied, equally as pleasantly, "I am. We were just discussing priorities. It's going to rain tomorrow," I added.

He nodded. "Sounds like today would be a good day

to be outside, then.”

By this time everyone was settling in around the fire, coffee cups in hand, trying to look attentive. Ignoring both Miles and me, Steele addressed the group.

“We’re going to spend the morning going over some basic survival skills,” he said, “including wilderness first-aid, fire-starting, building a shelter. After lunch, Miss Stockton will lead a wilderness excursion where you’ll get a chance to practice those skills.”

There were a few suppressed groans, and I looked at Steele, trying to hide my own surprise. I wondered where I was supposed to lead this excursion to.

“Right now,” Steele went on, “I’d like to turn your attention to the three priorities for survival that are written on the board. Miss Stockton is going to tell us why they are wrong.” He offered the marker to me, unsmiling.

Some people work hard at being a jerk; to others, it comes naturally. Steele was one of the latter. I took the marker from him and said politely, “Thank you, Mr. Steele.”

Miles winked at me, murmured, “Go get ’em, tiger,” and took his coffee to sit beside BJ on the sofa. Steele took a step back and watched me, expressionless, with his arms folded across his chest.

I said, “Actually there are five survival priorities and it’s important to keep them in order, especially in a crisis situation. I’m sure what Mr. Steele was thinking of with this list is the rule of three. Can anyone tell me what that is?" I glanced around the room and landed my gaze on Parker, one of the two people I was sure knew the answer. The other one was Miles, but I didn't think it would endear me to anyone to play favorites. "Parker?"

He said, "A person can survive three weeks without food, three days without water, and three hours in an extreme environment like heat or cold."

"Right." I drew the number one beside the word "shelter" and circled it. "So your first priority is shelter. Even if the environment is not what you'd call extreme at the moment, the weather can turn on you without warning. And keep in mind that if you're in a situation where you might have to go without food for a time, you'll get weaker every day, and building a shelter requires a lot of energy."

I drew a number two inside a circle beside the word "water" and said, "You always want to build your shelter close to a water source, but not so close you're in the path of predators who might also use that stream or pool. Always check for tracks." I erased the word "food" and wrote "fire" in its place. "Your water should be boiled for safety, and any fish or game you might bring in will have to be cooked."

I wrote "food" after that, and finally, number five, signaling. "Don't rely on your cell phone to get in touch with rescuers," I said. "As you've seen here, a lot of wilderness areas are out of reach of cell towers, and even under the best of circumstances, batteries die. But I'm sure Mr. Steele is going to cover all that." I smiled sweetly and returned the marker to him.

A round of applause followed me as Cisco and I went to take a seat on the rug in front of the stove. Parker made me blush with a shrill whistle of approval, but I personally thought all the approbation was more to annoy Steele than to demonstrate their appreciation of me.

To be honest, though, I felt bad for trying to show Steele up when, over the next couple of hours, he not only proved he knew his business, but actually taught me a thing or two. I was an amateur, and I knew it. Rick Steele did this for a living, and I respected that, I really did. It was just hard to show it when it was clear the man had no respect at all for any of us.

We spent the morning learning how to put together a rough lean-to from evergreen branches, and I picked up a few tips about wilderness first aid. I knew about using pine resin to disinfect wounds and seal minor scrapes but had never thought about using superglue to close deep gashes that would otherwise require stitches. I made a mental note to add superglue to my emergency kit.

We spent an hour outside practicing starting a fire without matches, with varying degrees of success. I moved from group to group, demonstrating how to cast a spark with the ferro rod from my multitool, and every time I stopped to help someone I had to wonder, *Is this the one? Is this the person who stole from the company and betrayed Miles?* Was it Theo, working so earnestly with steel and flint that drops of sweat beaded on his forehead, or Reed, making jokes about setting himself on fire? Neither seemed a likely candidate, but both had crossed an ocean and hiked five-miles, jet-lagged, just to make sure they were here this week. Could it be BJ, sleek and sophisticated and groaning about breaking a nail, or Max, who glumly declared that if her survival depended on building a fire with sparks and dried grass she would say her goodbyes now? Maybe it was Parker, who took time to scratch Cisco's chin and ask him how he was doing after the previous night's big adventure, and who then volunteered to coach Max on keeping her tinder going long enough to transfer it to her fire circle. The truth was, it was hard to imagine any of them being desperate enough, or conscienceless enough, to sell stolen technology, and what could they possibly need the money for? They all held jobs that paid more per year than I was likely to make in a lifetime. Why risk it all for something like this?

I was reminded, once again, that these people, as nice as they seemed, lived in a world I couldn't comprehend and would never be able to navigate. I couldn't even begin to imagine the things that motivated them.

We broke for lunch with instructions to assemble on the porch of the lodge in one hour. It was once again chaos in the kitchen as everyone tried to put together their own sandwiches and chips. With food dropping everywhere and feet shuffling back and forth, it was clearly no place for a dog. I hastily slapped together some ham and cheese and got out of there, signaling to Miles that I'd be out front.

On the way out, Ian stopped me with a grin.

"I have to say your presentation was a lot more interesting than Mr. Steele's. He doesn't have much of a personality, does he?"

I shrugged and glanced around but didn't see Steele. I had been raised not to speak ill of someone behind his back. "He knows his stuff," I said noncommittally.

"I think he's strange." This was from Parker, who reached between us to retrieve a paper plate. "One too many blows to the head, if you ask me. Where is he, anyway? Too good to eat with the plebes?" He obviously didn't expect an answer, because he grinned down at Cisco, whose eyes were glued to the lunchmeat Parker had just speared with his fork. "What do you think, buddy? This turkey looking good to you?"

I balanced my plate in one hand and tightened Cisco's leash with the other.

Ian said, "So where's this excursion going to take us this afternoon?"

Again I could do nothing but shrug. "I'm not in charge of the agenda. I'm sure it won't be far, though. The sun sets early this time of year."

Parker said to Ian, "Are you going? I wouldn't think you'd have to monitor every single minute of the course."

Ian replied, "It's what I signed up for. Besides, I enjoy the outdoors."

While they were talking, I slipped quickly away.

The temperature outside was milder now—58 degrees by my watch—and I settled on the steps of the porch in a patch of pale sunlight to eat my sandwich. Cisco stretched out beside me, watching with hopeful eyes. When the door opened behind us, he leapt to his feet, tail wagging madly, and I looked around, expecting Miles. BJ said, "Mind if I join you?"

I swallowed quickly and told Cisco, "Down!"

Cisco stretched out his paws on the floorboards reluctantly, watching BJ with an exuberant grin. BJ, apparently taking this as consent, sat beside me. She was wearing designer jeans with her hiking boots and a tucked-in red turtleneck sweater that showed off her figure. The jeans were completely impractical for winter hiking: the fabric was too thin to insulate or protect her legs from thorns and sharp branches and would take forever to dry if it got wet. The sweater was cute but too heavy to layer. She would have been better off with a thermal undershirt, like I wore, topped by a flannel shirt and puffer vest.

She glanced over at Cisco with a smile. Most people can't help smiling when they look at a golden retriever; Rick Steele was the obvious exception. "Does he have to stay tied to you like that all the time?"

"Not usually." I didn't think it was necessary to bring up last night's missing dog debacle, or the multiple acts of mischief he'd performed before that. "But I like to keep him close to me when we're in a strange place."

She nodded, spearing a piece of lettuce with her fork. There was nothing on her plate but last night's leftover salad, which hadn't been all that good when it was fresh, and a single oatmeal cookie. Someone should probably point out to her that restricting calories on a survival exercise was not the smartest move, but that someone would not be me. I took another bite of my sandwich.

"So how did you learn so much about wilderness survival?" BJ asked. "Not by experience, I hope, like Miles."

I replied, "I grew up in the mountains. It's something you just pick up." But I was more interested in what she'd said about Miles. "Although I got a lot of experience hiking the Appalachian Trail, just like Miles."

"Oh, yeah? How far did you get?"

"Virginia," I admitted. "And I started in North Carolina. So not that far."

"I'm sure Miles has told you he went the whole damn way. He's always been such an overachiever."

I smiled at that, and she added, "But that's not where he learned all the survival stuff. I think that happened while he was in military intelligence."

I stopped with my sandwich halfway to my mouth. "He was in military intelligence?"

Too late I realized how stupid that made me sound. How could I not know something so basic about the man I was going to marry?

BJ politely pretended not to notice my gaffe. "So I understand. He doesn't talk a lot about his past, as you've probably noticed." She took a bite of her salad and went on, "I guess he told you we dated. Of course he did. He's the most annoyingly honest man I've ever known. It wouldn't even occur to him that having his new fiancée and an old girlfriend spend a week together might be uncomfortable for one or the other of them."

She shrugged and smiled sympathetically, prompting a small smile from me in return. She seemed nice. I'd like to think that Miles only dated nice women, but I'd met some of his exes and knew that was not strictly true.

BJ went on, "Of course, we were far too much alike to ever make a go of it. But we parted friends, I married a pilot, had two amazing kids, and eventually, I came to work for him. We make much better colleagues than lovers. Oh, wait."

She reached into her back pocket and brought out her phone, putting her plate on the porch beside her. Cisco watched it with interest, and I watched Cisco. "Here," she said, scrolling through some screens. "I bored everyone else with these last night. Your turn." She passed the phone to me. "The fam."

The photo was of a good-looking man in a pilot's uniform and two gorgeous children, a boy and a girl, who looked to be around five or six. I wasn't sure whether she showed me the photo to reassure me she was not still interested in Miles, or because she was simply proud of her kids. Either way, it was a nice thing to do, and I found myself hoping that the spy in our midst, whoever it was, wasn't her.

"Twins," she explained, reaching over to scroll to another picture, this one of the two kids dressed in white holding Easter baskets. In the next one, they were sitting on a picnic blanket in the grass with BJ in between, an arm around each child. "We tried six years to have just one, and we ended up with two. Life is funny, huh?"

She scrolled through a dozen or more photos, narrating each one, and when I'd had enough cuteness, I politely returned the phone. "They're beautiful."

"Do you have any children, Raine?"

I shook my head. "I have dogs."

She laughed. "They're probably less trouble."

"And," I added, "just as adorable."

Cisco chose that moment to prove me wrong. Just as BJ went to pick up her plate he darted for her cookie and swallowed it whole without disturbing a leaf of lettuce. She stared at her plate in astonishment, and I jerked Cisco back, exclaiming, "I'm so sorry! Let me get you another cookie."

I started to get up, but she laughed, waving me down. "I didn't need it anyway." She put the plate down—on her other side, this time, well away from Cisco—and added, "You don't remember, but we've met before. After Melanie's mother died, I was at the house."

I said, "Oh." I didn't remember. That had been such a dark, confusing time, with dozens of lawyers and all sorts of other important people coming and going for days on end. I really didn't remember much of any of it.

"I told Miles then," she went on, "that you were the real deal and not the kind of girl to play around with. Do you know what he said to me?"

I did not, but I knew Miles. "Mind your own business?" I suggested.

She chuckled. "Close. He said, 'Do you think I don't know that?' And *then* he said, 'Mind your own damn business.' The point is, you're exactly the kind of woman Miles needs. It's just a shame it took him so long to find you."

"Oh, I don't know about that," I demurred. "I've met some of his exes. We don't have much in common."

"Precisely," she said. "Which is why they—we—are exes." She sat back, leaning her weight on her hands. "I've known Miles for twenty years, met every one of his wives and most of the girlfriends that hung around for more than a month. He was never as easy around them as he is around you. He never smiled at them the way he smiles at you. It's like all these years he's been pretending, and now he's not anymore." She gave me an encouraging smile. "Some of these guys gossip more than housewives, and just in case you overheard anything, I want you to know that the expert—that's me—couldn't approve more."

I couldn't help wondering what the "guys" had said about me, even though I was sure it was nothing I hadn't already said about myself. Miles Young with a country girl? Miles Young with a *dog trainer*, of all things? They probably gave it six months. That's why no one had been particularly excited to hear about the engagement. They didn't expect me to be around long enough for a wedding. And while I appreciated BJ going out of her way to reassure me, I also resented it a little. And I wasn't all that reassured.

I gave a small shrug. "That's nice of you to say, BJ, it really is. But I know Miles and I come from different worlds, and as crazy as I am about him, sometimes I think I don't know him at all." I shrugged again, embarrassed. I don't usually make personal revelations to people I don't know.

BJ placed a sympathetic hand on my knee. "Honey," she said, "trust me when I tell you that you are never going to know everything there is to know about Miles Young. But that's part of his charm, isn't it? Case in point," she added, a little too casually, "the last place I ever expected to see Miles was at this retreat. What in the world made him decide to come, do you suppose?"

Damn it. Just when I had almost eliminated her as a suspect, she had to start pumping me for information. Because of course if you were planning to use this retreat as a cover to sell corporate secrets, the boss's unexpected appearance would definitely make you nervous.

I smiled and replied easily, "You know Miles. Because he can, I guess." I gave Cisco's leash a small tug and got to my feet. "Excuse me, BJ. I've got to find Mr. Steele and see where I'm supposed to be leading the afternoon excursion. By the way," I added at the door, "you'll probably want to change into your hiking pants, just in case we hit rough country. Nice chatting with you."

She returned a quick smile of thanks for the advice that didn't seem entirely genuine, and I closed the door behind me, leaving her sitting alone.

CHAPTER EIGHTEEN

Rick Steele had a gun.

The door to his room was open a crack and I paused outside it, my hand raised to knock on the frame. His back was to the door as he pulled on his jacket, and I clearly saw a back holster clipped to his belt containing a subcompact pistol. He reached for his day pack and saw me standing there.

"Help you, Stockton?"

I said, "I thought you said no firearms were allowed."

"I did." He strode toward the door, and I had to step back quickly to avoid getting knocked over.

"But you have one."

"I also have a sat phone and an emergency kit that contains two preloaded morphine syringes. Do you have a problem with that?"

Any response I made would have sounded foolish,

because of course a man who was leading a survival course deep in the wilderness with the nearest medical or other assistance at least an hour away would have those supplies. If I had been responsible for protecting eight other people way out here, I probably would have carried a gun, too.

Still, it made me uneasy.

I increased my pace to keep up with him, Cisco trotting happily at my side. "I need to know the route we're taking this afternoon."

"We'll follow Dead Man's Trail a couple of klicks east, practice making camp at Overlook Ridge, then proceed north to Stone Road, which loops back to the lodge. Get your gear and meet out front. We leave in ten minutes."

I wanted to protest that sounded like an awful lot of territory to cover in one afternoon, but then I wasn't entirely sure what a "klick" was. Besides, I was pretty sure he would leave without me if I was late, so I veered off back to the bunk room. I grabbed my jacket and my day pack, strapped Cisco into his saddlebags, and arrived on the front porch at about the same time everyone else did.

There was a wooden picnic table at one end of the porch, upon which were several plastic shopping bags and a breadbasket from the kitchen. Steele stood beside the table, and without preamble said, "This afternoon's lesson is about the most important survival tool you have at your disposal: your mind. Stockton, what's the biggest mistake people make when they're lost in the wilderness?"

There were so many of them that I actually panicked for a moment trying to come up with the right answer. Everyone turned to look at me. Miles took a step closer to me and I felt his fingers lightly on the back of my neck. I said, "They panic."

Without acknowledging the rightness or wrongness of my answer, Steele turned back to the group. "Don't panic," he said. "Remember what you've learned. Make good decisions. Last night you all made some decisions. Today we'll see how good they were."

I saw now that each of the plastic shopping bags had someone's name written on it. Steele picked up one, glanced at it, and said, "Sandoval."

Parker came forward and Steele handed him the bag. Parker glanced inside, grinned, and brought out a minibar-sized bottle of vodka. "Half a dozen bottles of this, five bags of cashews, three plastic trash bags," he said. "Looks like my decision-making skills are pretty good."

Everyone laughed, and Steele held up another bag. "Valentine."

BJ came forward to receive her hand sanitizer, compact mirror, and sewing kit. Miles got a bag of tortilla chips and a package of socks. I began to understand that the point of the exercise today would be to put the items they had chosen last night to practical use. When it was my turn, I showed Steele the multitool I kept zipped inside my vest pocket and received a box of tampons in return.

"Leave your day pack here," Steele said. He nodded toward Cisco. "What's in his saddlebags?"

"Collapsible plastic bowls, dehydrated dog food, a reward toy, and two bottles of water," I said.

"Hand it over," Steele said.

"No," I replied. For emphasis, I drew Cisco a little closer to my knee. "I chose my dog as one of my survival items. In a real-life situation, I would never take him anywhere without food and water, and his saddlebags are always packed. He goes as is."

Steele's jaw knotted, causing the scar along the side of his face to pop, but he clearly couldn't think of an argument for that, at least not one that would appease me—or the man who had hired him. I left my pack on the table and moved away as he held up another bag. "Hodges," he called, and Max came forward.

When everyone had picked up their assigned items, Steele said, "For those of you who've been paying attention, today's exercise should be fairly easy. You've got good weather—which I don't have to remind you wouldn't necessarily be the case in a crisis situation—and the walk is level. We'll hike a few miles up Dead Man's Trail, you'll use the items in your bags and the skills you've learned to demonstrate the five"—he emphasized the word slightly as he glanced at me— "survival priorities. I'll meet you there. Miss Stockton will be your guide. I think she has some bushcraft techniques to share, and her dog might even do a few tricks for you."

There were a few weak smiles, but I could tell no one really thought it was funny. I certainly didn't.

Steele's gaze traveled over the group until he found Ian. "Mr. Wharton, since you indicated last night you didn't intend to participate in the exercise, I assume you'll be staying behind."

"Not at all," Ian said gamely. "I'm here to observe and observe I will. What's one more hike in the woods?"

"What, indeed?" murmured BJ, and when inquisitive gazes turned her way, she responded defensively, "What? I *love* the outdoors." I noticed that she had followed my advice and changed into hiking pants.

Steele said, "Okay, we're burning daylight. Leave your phones here in the basket and meet at the metal outbuilding to your left. If anybody needs to hit the head, now's the time."

I shot a quick look at Miles, trying to disguise my alarm. Without his phone, how could he monitor the tracking device? Any chance we had of devising a plan was now completely shot.

Parker said, "Why do we have to leave our phones? There's no service. What difference does it make?"

"Phones do a lot more than make calls and connect with the internet," Steele said. "They can be used as flashlights and compasses, as cameras, even signaling devices under the right circumstances. Mr. Carter was the only one who thought to grab his phone as a survival tool, so he's the only one who will be taking one along."

Theo grinned. "Take that, suckas."

"Yeah, well, I hope you enjoy using your passport to start a fire," retorted Max, dropping her phone into the basket.

"And I understand the squirrels around here are very open to bribes," added Reed, "so those credit cards will come in handy." He placed his phone in the basket and said to Steele, "Seriously, you *will* be locking these in the building, won't you?"

"My entire life is on this phone," BJ added, "not to mention 136,000 pictures of my babies."

"Your phones will be secure," Steele replied.

Listening to them joke and grouse, they all sounded so ordinary. Likeable, even. They were exactly the kinds of people Miles would hire and trust. It was hard to imagine one of them was involved in corporate espionage. But it wasn't hard at all to imagine the depth of the betrayal Miles must feel, knowing it was true.

I deliberately did not look at Miles as I said, "I downloaded the trail maps to my phone. I'll need them for navigation."

Steele responded with no noticeable change of expression. "Most wilderness guides can navigate a trail without a map."

I sucked in a sharp breath but released it when I felt Miles's calming hand on my back. The truth was, I had memorized the general contours of all the trails on the drive up here, so I wouldn't be entirely helpless without a map. But Steele didn't know that, and it was clear that, once again, he was just trying to trip me up.

Miles dropped his phone into the basket without protest, and in a moment, so did I.

Miles said, "No offense, Mr. Steele, but I think everyone would feel better if a couple of us went with you to make sure these are securely locked away. You're right. A phone is more than a way to access the internet, and there's a lot of personal information in that basket."

"Not a problem." Steele held out the basket to Ian as he moved past the table. "Mr. Wharton? If you're going on the hike, leave your phone behind."

Ian hesitated and I thought he would refuse, which would have been perfectly reasonable of him. He wasn't participating in the program or being held responsible for any of the exercises, and the whole thing seemed like more of a power play on Steele's part than a reasonable requirement. But after a moment, Ian shrugged and put his phone in the basket, most likely having reached the same conclusion as everyone else: without a service connection, the phone was worthless anyway.

To everyone except Miles.

CHAPTER NINETEEN

Trying to organize a group of high-level executives who are more accustomed to giving orders than taking them is roughly the equivalent of taking a basket of puppies to church. While Parker, Miles, and Steele went to secure the phones and lock the lodge, BJ and Max decided to go to the ladies' room. Theo and Ian forgot their jackets and went back to the lodge to get them. Reed got tired of waiting and went to hurry the others along. When Steele arrived at the rendezvous point, I was the only one there.

"All right, Stockton, it's all yours," he said. "I'll meet you at Overlook Ridge in a couple of hours." He pointed to a sign a few dozen yards away. It was shaped like an arrow with the words "Dead Man's Trail" clearly burned into it. "The trail," he said, deadpan, "is that way."

"Got it," I replied, equally deadpan, and he turned and strode away.

Actually, it suited me just fine to have Steele out of the way. When Miles and Parker arrived a few minutes later, I said, "Could one of you please see what's keeping the others? Steele is getting ahead of us."

As I spoke, I looked straight at Parker, so he had no choice but to reply, "Sure thing." He walked back toward the lodge, cupping his hands around his mouth and calling, "All right, everybody! Mount up! We're on the road in thirty seconds."

I grasped Miles's arm and whispered, "Did you get it?"

"Get what, sugar?"

"Your phone!"

He shook his head. "No need."

Before I could question, he pushed up the sleeve of his jacket, tapped a screen on his watch, and turned it toward me. A replica of the satellite view I had seen on his phone was displayed there, with the red dot still blinking over the lodge.

I smiled wryly. "They're linked," I said. "Your watch and your phone."

"Naturally. Makes it easier all around."

I said, "I'd like to keep everyone together on the trail, but once we get to the stopping place I can take each of them off away from the others…"

"Or I can," he put in.

"Either way, it will show on your watch, right, when the tracking code moves away from the others?" I spoke quickly, because BJ and Max were only a half-dozen yards away, with the men close behind. "And the rest is up to law enforcement, right? You'll have what you want to know, and that's the end of your involvement. We can leave."

He saw the anxiety in my eyes and put a reassuring arm around my shoulders, giving me a quick hug. "Don't worry, sugar."

I did not have a chance to respond because Max and BJ were upon us.

"I guess this is the place," BJ said cheerfully, gesturing toward the sign.

Max added, "This isn't a complaint, Chief, but if I'd known physical fitness was a requirement for this job, I might have spent more time at the gym."

"Relax, Hodges," said Reed, coming up behind them. "If it had been, I wouldn't have made it past the first interview."

Miles grinned and opened his bag of tortilla chips, offering it to him. "Snack?"

"Don't mind if I do," replied Reed, and helped himself to a couple of chips.

I wondered how Miles could be so relaxed, knowing that one of these people was a thief. And what was I doing, going off into the woods with them with no weapon, no radio, and no way to call for help?

Suddenly I was in a hurry to catch up with Steele.

CHAPTER TWENTY

Jessup slept the sleep of the completely conscienceless and awoke refreshed and curious. It occurred to him that the group at the lodge might present more opportunities than challenges for him, and those opportunities were definitely worth exploring.

Like most nomadic creatures, Jessup preferred to spend the winter months in warmer climates, and the time for his migration south was fast approaching. He would need supplies for the journey and his plan of provisioning from the stores of the abandoned lodge was no longer practical. But there were other ways he might take advantage of the situation.

He had made his camp in a stand of spruce overlooking the lodge, and he spent the morning watching the comings and goings below through his binoculars. He now knew there were nine people:

three women and six men. One of them—probably the leader—was armed. There was one vehicle. Their gear, for the most part, looked expensive and unused. Rookies, then.

He watched them throughout the morning, fumbling around trying to build a fire with damp wood, pretending to construct a shelter with fallen branches and evergreen they gathered from the surrounding woods. Even the dog, safely tied up on the porch out of the way, looked amused as he watched them work. A couple of them looked like they knew what they were doing. The others played at being pioneers like it didn't matter whether they succeeded or not, which was a huge mistake. In the wilderness, it *always* mattered.

Patience was not only a virtue but a tool, and Jessup watched the lodge without tiring as possibilities formed in the back of his head. Buzzards began to circle in the distance, but they did not worry him. It was doubtful anyone in the group would even notice, much less be motivated to follow them to their destination. Finally, an hour or two after noon, the group started down Dead Man's Trail—or at least most of them did. The big man, the leader, got into the car and drove away. The lodge was empty.

He noticed none of them carried packs, which meant they wouldn't be gone long. Whatever he was going to do, he would have to do it quickly.

Jessup had the advantage over the hikers because he could cover the distance in half, or even a quarter, of the time. He jogged through the woods, avoiding the trail, and reached the spot where his truck was hidden in less than an hour. He donned the park ranger's hat and jacket, just in case he happened to meet someone, and drove back to the lodge. There he pried the padlock off the garage door and poured two five-gallon cans of gas into the truck's tank. He might not need it, depending on how things worked out, but only a fool would undertake any venture without backup.

A less clever man, even a less experienced one, might have broken into the lodge and ransacked the guests' possessions for cash, credit cards, electronics, and other items that could be sold. He would have loaded up his provisions from the larder and been on his way. He very likely would have gotten away with it. But that would have been clumsy and careless. The problem with carelessness was that it could so very easily become a habit. One small stupid chance led to another bigger, stupider chance. And the longer a man got away with it, the lazier and more careless he became.

Jessup was a strategic man. He took his time, and he weighed his options. And he always, always knew what he was up against. The park ranger had been an unexpected complication that might have flustered a lesser man, led him into poor judgment, and caused him to make mistakes. But for Jessup, the unexpected simply became an imperative not to be caught off guard again.

He drove his truck down the service road and around to the parking spot at the bottom of the trail that led to the lodge, where it could remain without suspicion as long as the group was in the lodge. He reprovisioned his pack with all the necessities, including several different kinds of weapons and ammo, and began the walk back up the mountain. He might indeed return to the lodge and avail himself of whatever he needed there. But first, he had reconnaissance to do.

CHAPTER TWENTY-ONE

Dead Man's Trail was nothing like the steep, rocky climb we'd taken to get here. The path was wide and flat, carpeted in dried pine straw and lined with tall pines and graceful blue spruces. The view into the surrounding woods was unfettered by scrub or tangled brush, and I could tell by the slope of the land that the trail followed the path of a stream somewhere just out of view. It was so perfect that I wouldn't have been surprised to discover the park service used this view to promote the natural beauty of the park, and for the first couple of hundred yards or so even the grumpiest of the group were impressed.

Cisco and I took the lead, and I put Cisco on his long tracking leash so that he could go at his own pace while the others maintained a more leisurely stroll. Miles brought up the rear. Occasionally I'd point out local flora and their specific uses, but there wasn't a whole lot to be had this time of year. Reed asked if Cisco and I had ever been on a manhunt, and I told him that, while we frequently assisted in missing-person searches, the police did not solicit the assistance of amateurs on criminal manhunts.

I took this opportunity to turn and explain to the group, "One of the mistakes lost people make is they always move down. Downhill is easier, and people usually assume downhill will lead to a path or a road. The smart thing to do is to move up. You have a better line of sight from higher ground and a better chance of your signal being spotted. Also, scent drifts down, so search dogs will have a better chance of picking up your trail."

"That assumes, of course," Parker pointed out, coming to walk beside us, "that you want to be found."

"Right," I agreed. "But the truth is, if you've got a good search dog after you, there's not a whole lot you can do to avoid detection."

"Here's hoping the bad guys don't know about search dogs, then," Theo said.

"You can always throw your wallet at them," Reed returned.

Max called forward, "Don't you think we've gone far enough? How much longer?"

I was embarrassed to admit I did not know where the rendezvous point was; I assumed we would find it when we came to it. This irritated me, but I tried not to let it show as I replied, "Steele had a specific place in mind. I think we'd better stick with his plan."

Although I privately decided that if we did not find him within the next half hour or so, we would turn back. Dusk would overtake us before we reached the lodge otherwise, and twilight in the thick woods was no joke, especially without a flashlight.

I added, "And remember, the point of this exercise is to simulate making camp. So far, we haven't seen a place that would make a good campsite. But keep your eyes open."

"You know," said Parker, "generally this kind of exercise comes at the end of the course, not the beginning. Kind of a test of what you've learned."

I shrugged my agreement. "This is not the way I would have done it," I admitted. "But maybe the idea is for everyone to see what skills they need to work on."

I stopped, peering at the glint of something in the woods on the downhill slope of the trail. Cisco, sensing something interesting, trotted back to me from the length of his ten-foot leash and looked down the hill as well. I gathered up his leash and we stepped off the trail. As I looked closer, I discovered it was a bunch of somethings—dozens of empty soda cans, scattered across the ground near a stand of laurel bushes.

"Oh, good heavens," said BJ at my shoulder. "Look at that mess. Who does something like that in such a beautiful place?"

"A bear, most likely," I said. It looked as though a camper or a ranger had gathered up their recycling and had forgotten to secure it before a curious bear came along. I was pretty sure I'd find a shredded garbage bag tangled up in the undergrowth nearby.

"Bear?" Max sounded alarmed. "Nobody said anything about bears!"

"Don't worry," I said. "Most bears around here are inactive this time of year. This probably happened last spring." I turned to the group and added, "Where there are humans, there will be trash. You need to keep your eyes open for things like this. They can usually be found downhill, like this, or near water, where they've been washed downstream. Pick up as many of these cans as you can fit into your bags. What we don't use we'll pack out."

BJ frowned. "Now we're on trash duty?"

I had started down the slope, Cisco close to my side, but now I looked back. "Did anyone bring a metal container to boil water in?" At their confused silence, I pointed downhill. "Metal containers."

Cisco barked what might have been interpreted as agreement, but when I looked at him I saw his ears were pricked and his nostrils twitching. He had caught the scent of something below, and I looked around uneasily before proceeding. Not *all* bears were inactive this time of year.

Miles touched my arm. "Come on, babe, we can handle it. No point in everyone getting muddy."

I started to object because the point of the camp was to teach *them* self-reliance, not us. But I was starting to worry about the lateness of the hour, and I knew the whole thing would go a lot faster if Miles and I did it ourselves. So I said, "Okay, take five, everyone."

The words were met with groans of relief. They

found places to sit on the ground, working out kinks in elbows and shoulders. Parker passed around a bag of cashews, and Max grudgingly shared what was left of her bottle of water. I gathered up enough shopping bags to hold all the cans, and Cisco, Miles, and I made our way down the slope, sliding on pine straw and mud slicks, until we reached the spill of aluminum cans.

I looped Cisco's long leash around the bare branches of an elderberry bush, and he immediately moved off, nose to the ground, eagerly tracking whatever had caught his attention from the trail above. I watched him curiously for a moment, and then Miles said, "Look at those buzzards."

His head was tilted toward the sky, and I followed his gaze toward the north where an enormous flock of buzzards—two dozen or more—circled the treetops. "Wow," I said, "must be something big."

I bent to pick up a can and added in a lower voice, "Is your tracker still on target?"

"Yep." He did not look up, and he kept his voice as low as mine even though it was clear from the sounds of conversation above us that no one was paying attention to what we were saying. "Right with us."

"So you were right. He wouldn't leave it in a backpack."

"Or she," he corrected.

I agreed worriedly, "Right." Maybe I should have spent more time interrogating BJ, instead of letting her interrogate me.

I was distracted by Cisco pawing at the ground

a few yards away and was afraid he might have uncovered more trash of the kind that would go straight into his mouth. I said sharply, "Cisco, leave it." He promptly stepped back and sat down, his eyes fixed on the ground. He can be remarkably obedient when no one is watching.

I went to see what had attracted his attention, expecting something nasty—a dead raccoon or a package of rotten meat from the trash bag. I wasn't that disappointed. The patch of leaves Cisco had been pawing was matted and dark with blood. There were more blood spatters a few feet away. I motioned to Miles, and he joined me. He bent down and touched the bloody patch, rubbing one of the leaves between his fingers.

"Congealed," he said. "Probably happened yesterday sometime."

"Deer?" I suggested.

"Maybe." He pointed to the slope of the bank where there were clear drag marks, also spattered with blood. "Looks like he claimed his kill. And if he field-dressed it and tossed away the offal up ahead, that would explain the buzzards."

"Is it deer season here?"

He shook his head. "I don't know. But it doesn't matter. This far out, on private land, the last thing a hunter would worry about is being caught."

I looked at him skeptically. "What do you mean you don't know? I thought you knew everything."

"I don't know everything," he corrected, "Google does. And being currently Google-less..." He shrugged. "I'm completely helpless."

At another time, the thought of Miles being completely helpless would have made me smile. But out here alone standing on a patch of bloody ground, it didn't seem so funny. I pulled Cisco closer and looked around uneasily. "I don't like the idea of being out here with hunters around. Steele didn't say anything about that."

"Yeah, I'm not crazy about it either. We're probably okay this time of day—most hunting takes place at dawn—but let's keep our eyes open. And tell the others to be careful."

We gathered up the remaining cans quickly and started back up the hill.

The climb up the hill was harder than it had been going down. I slipped once, falling hard on one knee, and my hiking watch buzzed. A message scrolled across the screen: *Fall detected. Push side button three times for emergency assistance.* I swiped away the screen impatiently, but suddenly I missed Casey. I missed Melanie and the Aussies and my farmhouse and waking up every morning to do ordinary chores —feeding the dogs, cleaning the kennels, checking e-mails. I missed Dog Daze and my colorful training room decorated with the ribbons I'd won and the trophies I'd earned and the pictures of all the dogs who'd graduated from one of my courses. I wanted to get back to work. I wanted to go home.

"Okay, babe?" Miles took my arm to help me to my feet.

I caught his jacket to steady myself, and I looked

earnestly into his eyes. "Miles," I said, "I don't want you to go to South America anymore. Or the Middle East, or Eastern Europe, or any place like that."

His smile seemed a little indulgent. "Okay."

I tightened my hand on the fabric of his jacket as he started to resume the climb up the hill. "Is that okay you agree, or okay you heard me?" It was important to be precise with Miles.

"It means I hear you, sweetheart," he returned gently. "I always hear you." He put his hand on my back to give me an assist up the hill. "Come on. Let's go."

I knew by that it was pointless to tell him what I really wanted: to leave all this intrigue in the hands of the professionals, and simply go home.

CHAPTER TWENTY-TWO

The trail began to narrow and dip slightly as we moved farther along, following the course of a winding stream whose noisy waters sounded closer with every turn. Occasionally the woods would open up to reveal a vast view of layered blue mountains, reminding us of how high we really were. At one point the trail narrowed to a pass of less than three feet wide, with a sheer drop of at least thirty feet down a rocky cliff on one side. It looked like the result of a recent landslide, and I wondered if Steele had even known about it when he plotted this route. I held my breath until everyone, including Cisco, made it safely across.

Less than an hour later we came upon a curve in the trail. To the left was a mossy bank that led to a wide, bubbling stream. To the right, the land opened up onto a flat glade dotted with spruce and pine trees, beyond which was a postcard view of the cloud-topped Smoky Mountains. Overlook Ridge. Rick Steele sat on a fallen log, watching our approach. Beside him was a bundle, maybe two by four feet, covered in a blue tarp.

He stood and glanced at his watch. "Took your time, didn't you, Stockton?"

"I didn't know it was a race."

Cisco, seeing Steele, had immediately tried to bound forward to greet him, but I pulled him back, unclipping his long tracking leash and replacing it with the bungee leash clipped to my pants. While the others wandered up, dropping their bags of aluminum cans and other allotted items, I took one of the collapsible bowls from Cisco's pack and filled it with bottled water. He lapped it up quickly, more interested in exploring the new area than he was in personal comfort.

Steele raised his voice to address the group. "All right, people. First priority is shelter. Pick your campsite. You're looking for a site that's sheltered from the wind but away from trees with dead limbs. You will be building a lean-to capable of protecting you from rain and wind. You will be constructing a heating fire and a cooking fire. Your cooking fire should not be close to your sleeping area. Why? Because predators are attracted by the remnants of human food that might fall into the fire or around it. You will be collecting water and making it potable. You will find a way to feed yourselves or go hungry. You will do all this using the items you have brought with you. Any questions?"

Max said incredulously, "You want us to do all this *now*? Can't we rest first?"

"You can do whatever you like," replied Steele. "But…" he glanced toward the sky. "You have less than two hours before full dark. I'd get to it if I were you." He turned to me. "Stockton, the trail joins up with Stone Road about 500 yards north. The lodge is about 10 klicks away. A vehicle will be waiting to transport you all there in the morning. Until then, you're in charge."

I managed, "Wait. What?" at about the same time his words registered with everyone else.

"Did you say morning?" someone demanded.

Another said, "You're not leaving us here?"

"You didn't say anything about spending the night out here! We don't even have our backpacks!"

Steele held up a hand to quiet the barrage of protests. "Out of consideration for your delicate natures," he said, "and taking into account the presence of your insurance rep, who'd have a stroke if any of you high-priced folk caught a cold, I'm leaving you a present."

He pulled back the blue tarp to display a pile of sleeping bags, neatly rolled and tied. They weren't the ones we'd brought with us to the lodge; I assumed he supplied them as part of the package.

"The temperature will remain above freezing tonight," he went on, "and no rain is expected until tomorrow. Nonetheless, I wouldn't waste any time getting your fires built. Good luck to you."

Without another word, he rolled up the tarp, tucked it under his arm, and walked back up the trail, headed toward the north.

There was a stunned moment of silence, then everyone spoke at once.

"Of all the outrageous…"

"He can't be serious!"

"This is crazy!"

"I don't think any of us signed up for this!"

"Are you kidding me? Overnight in the woods with no food or water or even a tent?" This was BJ. "Miles, really, this is too much. What if there's an emergency? We don't even have a radio! Really, this borders on reckless endangerment *and* malpractice. And if you don't fire him immediately, you're leaving yourself open to liability as well."

Reed said, "I say we're wasting time standing here arguing. Let's turn around and go back."

Miles looked at me. "Raine?"

I took a deep breath, clearing my head of the shock. S.T.O.P. Sit. Think. Observe. Plan. Maybe I should have expected this. I hadn't. Now we all had to figure out a way to deal with it.

I said, "If we go back the way we came we're probably going to be on the trail after dark. A bad idea under any circumstances, and especially without flashlights."

"I have my phone," Theo insisted. "We can use the app."

I shook my head. "It won't be bright enough out here, and I'm not sure the battery will last until we get to the lodge."

I looked up the trail the way Steele had gone. "We could try following him."

"Yes," said Max quickly. "Let's do that."

I looked at Miles. I don't claim we are always in sync by any means, but there are certain times—especially when it's important—when I know exactly what he is thinking. A slight shift of his gaze, or an almost imperceptible shake of his head, told me he did not think that was a good idea. And he was probably right.

"But," I went on, "without a topographical map I don't know what condition that road he was talking about is in, or if it's even a road at all. I remember it did loop back to the lodge, but we might have to cross water or do some climbing, and what the hell is a klick, anyway?"

"About half a mile," Parker supplied. "So once we hit the road, we're still five miles from the lodge."

Amidst the chorus of groans, I looked at Ian glumly. "Well, I guess now we know why the insurance company wanted two instructors."

He held up a defensive hand. "Believe me, if I had known anything about this part of the plan, I'd still be back at the lodge playing Candy Crush on my phone. However," he added, glancing around the group, "if you don't mind me saying so—and I know I'm not really part of the class—but it seems to me we've already forgotten the first rule of survival. Don't panic."

He said it with a wry smile, and it was enough to cause some of the others to look a little shamefaced.

BJ scowled with embarrassment and irritation. "That son of a bitch," she muttered, "leaving us stranded out here in the middle of nowhere. And the worst part of it is, we signed a waiver!"

I said thoughtfully, "I don't think he did abandon us." At their curious glances, I explained, "Steele is a professional. He's not going to risk ruining his reputation by leaving a bunch of rookies in the woods in the middle of winter to fend for themselves. Also, how's he going to evaluate you if he can't observe how you react under stress? He knows there's at least one person with wilderness experience here, and two people with pretty good survival skills—Miles and Parker. So it's not as reckless as it appears."

Parker said, "I agree. This is all part of the exercise. He's planning to camp out there somewhere, close enough to keep an eye on us but far enough away that we feel like we're on our own. It's a sim test."

"He has a sat phone and a med kit," I added, "and he'll be close enough to respond in case of emergency. I'm betting on it."

But even as I spoke, I knew that I might be literally betting their lives. And why in the world hadn't I insisted he leave the phone and the med kit?

I watched their expressions change from mid-level panic to mild uneasiness as they glanced at each other. Miles, characteristically, said nothing, letting everyone reach the same conclusion as he had in their own time.

Theo said nervously, "Are you sure we can't make it back before dark?"

Max responded wearily, "Are you seriously up for turning around and doing that hike again before we've even had a chance to rest?"

"At least you've had water," Reed returned, somewhat resentfully. "And to answer your question, this is one person who's not up for it. Not without some hydration and a few minutes to catch my breath."

"I thought the plan was to hike out here, build a fire, take a shortcut back to the lodge," Theo said. "I could have handled that."

For a while everyone was quiet, considering their options. But they all knew there was only one voice that mattered, and eventually, all eyes turned to Miles. Even mine.

"Raine's right," he said. "It took us too long to get here to risk trying to turn around and go back now. This was obviously Steele's plan from the beginning, so we go with it. First priority," he said, "shelter. We'd better get to it."

I took the remaining bottle of water from Cisco's pack and handed it to Reed. Cisco had been vaccinated against giardia and leptospirosis, so he would actually be fine drinking from the stream. But it was hard to feel sorry for Reed, who had consumed more than his share of Miles's salty chips on the hike up here and surely knew that one consequence of salty snacks was thirst. "Share," I admonished him. "This will have to do until we get the fire started and can boil some water."

He unscrewed the cap and took a long drink

without bothering to thank me, and I turned to address the rest of the group. "It'll be faster if we work in teams," I said, my thoughts organizing efficiently now that the decision had been made. "Reed and Theo, look for lodge poles—fallen branches four to six feet long that we can use to build lean-tos. Miles and I will cut limbs from the spruce trees to use for roofing. Parker and Ian, collect some rocks from the creek for the fire rings. Ladies, start digging up moss and bringing it back here. It'll insulate the ground and act like a mattress for our sleeping bags. And start rinsing out those cans in the creek to carry water. We can do this if we work together."

CHAPTER TWENTY-THREE

I looped Cisco's leash around a pine sapling and gave him a Nylabone to chew while Miles and I stripped low-hanging branches from spruce and cedar trees to use for the shelters. Given our limited materials, we decided it would be more efficient to put together several small lean-tos, rather than try to erect one long one that would cover us all. There was a slight rise toward the east end of the glade, forming a rhododendron-covered bank that would make a perfect windbreak and also a solid back wall for our shelters. While I sawed at the limbs with my multitool, Miles dragged the piles of branches to the bank. The buzzards continued to circle overhead, adding exactly the kind of atmosphere we didn't need.

"He didn't have to take the tarp," I grumbled, tossing another armload of evergreen onto the pile. "We could have used that for a roof."

"I think that was the point."

"He's probably using it for his *own* roof." I glanced around, making sure we were alone, and lowered my voice. "He has a gun."

"Steele?"

I nodded. I pulled down another branch, then stopped and swiped the back of my arm across my damp forehead. My shoulders ached from working over my head to cut the branches, and I took a moment to rotate my neck, loosening the stiff muscles. "He's probably carrying it for defense against wildlife or maybe just because that's what you do in his job," I said. "It just struck me as odd."

"What kind of gun?"

"I didn't get a very good look. Some kind of subcompact semiautomatic handgun." I thought a minute and added, "It had an anchor on it."

Miles nodded. "Probably his service weapon from the SEALs. SIG Sauer P226, in case you're interested."

I grinned at him wearily. "I love it when you talk sexy to me."

Miles grinned back, the tight lines around his eyes relaxing momentarily. Then he said, sobering, "I had an idea about who might have let Cisco out last night."

I looked at him curiously. "Besides Steele?"

"He might not approve of dogs at the camp, but he didn't really have a motive. But somebody who was worried about a dog barking when he was trying to move quietly, or tracking him when he tried to get away..."

"Like whoever has your software code?"

"That person would be very nervous about having a tracking dog around," he pointed out.

I thought about Max, who had been so annoyed with Cisco yesterday—justifiably, maybe—and Parker, who had been so nice to him, and Reed and Theo and BJ, who had virtually ignored him, and tried to imagine which one of them could be so depraved they would take an innocent animal and lead him into the forest to die. The more I thought about it, the madder I became.

"Damn it," I muttered, sawing viciously at a branch. "What kind of sicko does something like that?"

Instead of answering, Miles let me work out my anger on half a dozen evergreen branches. When I paused, flushed and breathing hard, to swipe my arm across my face, he smiled at me.

"I like seeing you like this."

"Sweaty, dirty, and mad?" I was working in my thermal undershirt, my flannel shirt and my jacket tied around my waist, my hair a tangled mess, and my face streaked with dirt. But I guess he'd seen me look worse.

"Taking charge," he corrected. "Solving problems, getting things done. Doing what you do best."

He surprised me then by dropping his hands atop my shoulders and stepping in close, lowering his forehead to mine. His eyes filled my vision. He said somberly, "You're my hero, sugar, you know that. You always have been. I can't stand seeing you broken." He placed a tender, lingering kiss on my forehead. "I've missed you, Raine Stockton. It's time to get back to work."

With a puzzled, uncertain look, I turned away to grasp another branch.

He stopped me with a gentle hand on my arm. "That's not what I meant. Just… get back to being you, okay? We all need that. *I* need that."

I hesitated, searching his face, and I thought I was starting to understand what BJ had been trying to tell me earlier. About who Miles really was, and what he needed. I answered softly, "Okay."

He took the multitool from me and turned to start sawing at the branch I'd been holding. "Drag the rest of those branches back to the site, will you? I think we're pretty close to being done here."

CHAPTER TWENTY-FOUR

Jessup had counted nine of the intruders in total, with two camps. The high camp, the one boldly sheltered by a blue tarp, was perilously close to the partial remains of the park ranger, which could prove to be inconvenient for Jessup. He had watched the big man all afternoon and knew him to be a savvy woodsman, well-provisioned, and armed. He built a fire hot enough to give off almost no smoke and kept it fed with good, dry wood. He carried a canvas canteen of water, so he wouldn't have to go to the creek for it. He made his shelter against a solid windbreak and staked the tarp to the ground, not to tree limbs as so many amateurs tried to do. The others might be easy prey, but Jessup decided it was wisest to stay out of this man's path if at all possible.

Unfortunately, that would not remain possible for long.

Jessup set up his observation station directly across from the high camp with the blue tarp. He watched for over an hour as the man set up his camp, carrying supplies from the vehicle parked on the service road a quarter mile away. He watched him heat and eat an MRE, all the while using binoculars to observe the goings on at the camp in the glade below where the other eight intruders were.

Jessup was well disguised in the deep brush of the forest, even his binoculars dusted with a nonreflective coating, and he was not concerned about being detected. A common truth for hunters was that you rarely found what you weren't looking for, and the big man was too focused on the scene below to think about doing an in-depth search of the surrounding countryside.

But then, perhaps inevitably, the man's binoculars found something he had not been looking for.

Jessup watched as the intruder left his shelter and started down the slope into the woods, his eyes studying the forest floor beneath his feet. Jessup, as stealthy as a ghost, paralleled his movements, crossing on silent feet to move ever closer. When the man stopped, bent down, and touched something on the ground, Jessup raised his binoculars and saw the red stain on his fingers. The man continued to follow the blood trail, and Jessup continued to follow him.

He was a dozen yards from discovering for a fact what his view from the camp had only suggested when Jessup decided it was pointless to delay further. The buzzards screeched overhead, and when the man paused, craning his neck to look upward at them, Jessup took aim and let his arrow fly. The bolt severed the man's carotid with a gush of blood, and he collapsed like a sack of sand.

Once again, the unexpected had struck. And once again, Jessup had dealt with it quickly, decisively, and without panic.

He moved quickly through the woods to the fallen man. He took his gun from the holster and his knife from the scabbard. Both were nice weapons, and he coveted the SIG Sauer. But on further examination, he saw the anchor insignia and reluctantly dropped the gun to the ground. Too unique, too identifiable. He had plenty of weapons, and this one, if he were caught with it, could only mean trouble.

The dead man had $500 in cash in his pants pocket, and Jessup took that too. Everything else—keys, credit cards, ID—Jessup tossed deep into the woods. He had no use for any of those items, and their absence might make the body harder to identify when or if it was found.

And that, of course, was another problem. The body. The tools he customarily used for disposing of remains were locked away in his truck, and his truck was parked several miles away at the trailhead that led to Hidden Lodge. It would take him most of the night to get there and back, leaving the remaining eight campers completely unsupervised in the meantime. Who *were* those people? What were they doing here? The most obvious course of action open to him was to hike down to his truck and drive away. But could he really afford to do that without knowing the answers to those questions?

Jessup dragged the man's body a few dozen yards away behind the trunk of a large fallen tree and covered it with the broken branches of an evergreen. It was several hundred yards off the trail and the chances of anyone searching this deep into the woods were small, but a person couldn't be too careful.

He climbed the hill to the dead man's shelter and found the satellite phone he had seen in the man's pack earlier. He placed the instrument on a boulder, found another, heavier rock, and smashed it into its smallest electronic components. Then he gathered up as many of the pieces as he could and tossed them down the side of the hill, watching as they scattered among the dead leaves and forest debris. He found a med kit—always useful—and slung it over his shoulder by the strap. He was about to go through the pack when a movement down below caught his eye.

It was a woman. And the dog.

CHAPTER TWENTY-FIVE

When I'd met the members of Miles's elite corporate crew less than twenty-four hours ago, I would not have believed them capable of what I saw materialize over the next hour: two firepits, encircled with stones, four shelters lined with moss and roofed with a combination of Parker's trash bags and evergreen boughs lashed together with the paracord from the bracelet I wore around my wrist. We made fires with tinder formed from dried grass, shredded cotton tampons soaked in alcohol, and corn chips. I clipped the lids off the aluminum cans and soon enough water to accommodate the entire camp was simmering on the embers of the cooking fire. A respectable stack of firewood stood beside the shelter and the big fire ring in front of it.

"Not bad," I complimented them, surveying all they had accomplished. I smiled at Miles. "You've got a good team."

"Yeah, I do," he agreed, but his returned smile showed his mixed emotions. The words meant more than was apparent.

"I know we've got three weeks before we starve to death," BJ said, "but I'm not used to all this exercise in one afternoon and I'm here to tell you I'm about to starve to death."

"I'm with you, sister," Max said.

She sank heavily to the sleeping bag that was rolled up in front of one of the lean-tos, and BJ sat down beside her. The tops of their heads brushed the leafy roof of the shelter and BJ ran an unsteady hand through her hair. They both should have been wearing hats; forty-five percent of heat loss occurs through the head. I suspected the trembling in BJ's hand was from muscle fatigue and low blood sugar, but I graciously didn't say anything about the Weight Watchers salad she'd had for lunch. Particularly when I remembered the lost cookie.

Miles passed them his bag of tortilla chips, now almost empty since he'd been sharing them all afternoon. BJ took the bag gratefully. "I'm not proud," she said. She took a handful and shared the bag with Max.

Theo suggested, "Maybe you'd like to try catching some trout with your sewing kit, BJ." He helped himself to a chip from the bag.

BJ made a face, but it was a weary effort. "Maybe for breakfast."

I looked toward the north, where I had earlier

noticed a stand of bare oaks farther in the woods, not too far from our camp. "I have a better idea." I picked up one of the shopping bags we'd used to carry the soda cans. Cisco, who had been lying at my feet, hopefully watching BJ and Max pass the bag of tortilla chips back and forth between them, sprang to his feet. I snapped on his tracking leash. "Back in half an hour."

Miles started to come with me, but I waved him back. "No need," I said. "I'm just going up to the road to check it out."

"Protocol," Parker reminded me. "Don't leave camp without a buddy."

"That's why I'm taking Cisco," I told him.

The fact was, I wasn't going for an ordinary stroll, and I didn't want to be slowed down by either of the men. As soon as I was out of sight of the camp, I put Cisco into tracking mode and let him do his thing. I had to know which one of my theories was right. Had Steele, a responsible survival instructor, made camp a few hundred yards away so that he could keep an eye on us, or was he somehow involved in the conspiracy to sell proprietary technology and had gone back to the lodge in hopes of stealing the device that contained it?

As far as I knew only one person had gone this way today, and Cisco's nose should lead me right to him. I smiled in relief to realize I was right: after less than ten minutes on the trail, the wooded path opened up onto a dirt road marked with tire tracks. I realized this must be what Steele had called Stone Road, the service road that led back to the lodge and, presumably back to a main highway. This was how Steele had brought in the sleeping bags.

The circling buzzards seemed closer now, and there were a lot of them. The remains of whatever had died here were probably in the woods adjacent to our camp, and that made me uneasy. I let Cisco follow the scent trail a few hundred feet to a black Navigator that was parked on the side of the road, and from there, to a faint path marked by nothing more than the bent twigs of scrub brush and leaves that had been overturned to show their damp undersides. The land sloped upward, and when I followed the terrain, I thought I caught a glimpse of something blue deep within the tangle of evergreen and brush. The tarp. Of course, Steele would have made his camp on a rise so that he could look down on us, and the wind would carry the smoke from his campfire away. He was probably watching me now, binoculars to his eyes, ready to scold me for leaving my charges alone.

Cisco was anxious to follow the scent trail into the woods, pulling hard on the lead with his nose to the ground, but I had found what I wanted and wasn't in the least interested in a confrontation with Steele. I told Cisco, "Finish." I took out the rope toy I had tucked into my cargo pocket as a reward for a job well done. He played with it happily, but like any good tracking dog, wanted to complete the job. He kept turning back towards the scent trail. I reeled in his leash, winding it around my hand, and started back toward the dirt road. That was when I heard a stick snap sharply behind me.

I stopped, turning toward the sound. "Mr. Steele?" I scanned the woods behind me. "Is that you?"

Cisco's ears pricked and his head, too, was turned toward the sound. His tail started to wag, and he grinned a greeting, panting lightly. There was definitely someone out there, and it was someone he knew. I called again, "Hello?" Nothing but the friendly back-and-forth swishing of Cisco's tail.

The silence from the woods grew heavier, and I felt a chill rise on the back of my neck. I could sense someone's presence just as surely as Cisco could smell it. Would it kill him to answer me? I raised my voice to be heard. "Just foraging. Don't worry. I won't tell anyone you're here."

Nothing.

I waited a moment, scanning the woods, feeling his gaze, growing more and more creeped out. Then I gave Cisco's leash a quick tug and lost no time returning to the road.

CHAPTER TWENTY-SIX

There is, among all predators, the danger of a thing called bloodlust. It happens most often when the prey is bountiful and the killing easy. The rush of adrenaline becomes its own reward, the fear of failure fades, and the predator begins to believe itself invulnerable. Greed sets in, and soon after greed comes carelessness. Jessup was acutely aware of the dangers of bloodlust and was focused on carefully, constantly keeping it at bay.

That was what had caused him to remove his finger from the trigger of the crossbow when he sited the woman and her dog alone on the trail. Cut off from the herd. Easy prey. Too easy. And the dog was a problem, after all. He would have to be taken out sooner or later.

Jessup had been so close. A single, silent arrow would have felled the dog. Before the woman could even turn around, he would have let loose another killing bolt, right through the back of her neck. And it was at that moment, with his finger on the trigger, that he grew careless, stepped on a branch, and revealed his presence.

The dog recognized his scent, no doubt remembering the venison jerky. It wagged its tail and grinned that foolish, harmless grin and reminded Jessup that he was teetering on the edge of that most dangerous of conditions, a loss of control. When chances were taken just because they were there. When consequences were forgotten in the heat of wanting. When any action, no matter how ill considered, seemed like the right one.

He lowered his weapon silently. He let the woman and the dog pass unmolested.

That did not mean there weren't problems that remained to be dealt with. It simply meant he needed a strategy.

There was a chance none of them would venture far enough from the campsite to stumble upon his handiwork. In fact, from what he had observed so far, the odds were in his favor on that score. But the dog could be trouble, particularly if this turned out to be some kind of hunting expedition that would lead them all to spend tomorrow tramping through the woods. He hadn't seen any weapons, but who was to say they weren't stored in the vehicle he'd seen parked on the road or scheduled to be delivered later by someone else? He needed to be sure. He needed to make strategic decisions.

There was a difference between taking unnecessary chances and taking deliberate chances for a certain reward. He needed more information. Knowledge was his strongest ally, his sharpest tool. As long as he had information, he was in control.

It was time to take control.

CHAPTER TWENTY-SEVEN

I returned as dusk was settling with a shopping bag filled with the mushrooms I had cut from the bark of an old oak tree not far beyond the campsite. Thanks to a warm, wet autumn, they were still tender and edible.

"Chicken of the woods," I explained. "They grow on old oak trees like little fans in a row. Not much protein, but plenty of other vitamins and minerals. You can live on them for a good long while if you don't have any other options. They need to be washed and boiled."

BJ looked skeptical as I held up a handful. "Wild mushrooms?" she said. "Are you sure they're safe?"

"Are you kidding?" Miles took the bag from me. "You'd pay forty dollars a plate for these in any restaurant in DC. But we're not eating them boiled." He handed the bag to Theo. "Go wash these off in the creek. Parker, have you got any of those cashews left? Raine, let me see that fancy multitool of yours."

As Theo took the bag of mushrooms and started across the trail to the creek, Cisco suddenly sat up straight and barked. I caught his leash close to the collar and he barked again, his eyes focused on the trail. A look of unease went around the group and Theo stood still, looking up and down the trail.

Someone called, "Hello, campsite!"

Cisco's tail wagged in happy greeting as a figure appeared on the trail from the north, coming toward us in the dusk. Theo returned quickly to the fire and Miles and Parker stood up, instinctively moving a little apart and turning to face the stranger. I had seen Casey do much the same thing when faced with the unexpected: get to his feet, look for the danger, and ready himself for fight or flight. So, come to think of it, had my former husband, a cop. The difference between ex-military, ex-cop, and ex-con was really not all that much when it came right down to it.

The man stepped off the trail and into the perimeter of our campsite, stopping before he came close enough to be perceived as a threat—and also too far away for us to be able to tell much about him. He wasn't wearing a backpack, so he wasn't a hiker. He was a smallish man, wiry and thin, with a short, sharp, ginger-colored beard on a narrow face. As I looked closer I saw he was wearing a park ranger's uniform. A billed cap with the park service insignia covered his hair.

Miles said, "How're you doing?" His tone was

friendly, but he was assessing the stranger as carefully as I was.

The man jerked his thumb over his shoulder in the direction of the road from which I'd come not long ago. "I was just on my way home and saw your smoke," he said. "Thought I'd check and see if everything was all right. You must be the group from the lodge."

Parker, having noticed the uniform too, replied, "We're not on park service land. We were told open fires were allowed."

"Oh, sure, sure," the ranger replied. He nodded at Cisco with a grin. "Dogs, too. That's a fine-looking one, isn't he?"

Cisco, who was held tightly in a sit at my knee, swished his tail along the ground and grinned enthusiastically. I stared at the man's uniform, trying to figure out what was not quite right about it.

Max volunteered, "We're on a survival retreat. It's a corporate thing, training camp for executives. Apparently, we're expected to sleep under the stars and eat wild mushrooms."

He chuckled. "That's about the size of it, all right. I just wanted to make sure you knew there's another fellow up there on the ridge." Again he gestured over his shoulder in the direction from which he had come. "He's got a pair of binoculars and I think he's watching you."

"Steele," I told Miles. "I saw him when I was out looking for the mushrooms."

The alarm that had flashed on BJ's face faded to relief. "Our instructor," she told the ranger. "He's keeping an eye on us, which is good to know."

I wondered how the ranger had been able to see Steele from the road, and how he knew he had binoculars.

"How long are y'all planning to camp out here?" the ranger asked.

"Just overnight," Reed supplied. "Thank God."

Suddenly I realized what it was that bothered me about the ranger's uniform. And it made no sense at all.

"Well, y'all be careful if you go out exploring," the ranger said. "I noticed some hunters out here the last day or two, and you need to be wearing reflective vests. Especially"—he nodded to Cisco— "the dog."

"Don't worry about that," BJ assured him adamantly. "We're packing up first thing in the morning and heading back the way we came."

He smiled and nodded. "Just make sure your fires are out. Ashes should be cold to the touch when you leave. This time of year, wildfires get started awful easy up here."

"We'll be careful," Miles assured him.

Silence fell, and I got the feeling the man was sizing us up, one by one, much in the same way we had been studying him. I didn't like it.

Then he said, "Well, I'll let you get on with it. Y'all take care now."

He turned and walked back up the trail the way he had come. No one moved or spoke until he was completely out of sight. Then Parker said, "Did anyone besides me think that was weird?"

I said, "He was out of uniform." And when everyone looked at me, I explained. "No name tag. And," I added hesitantly, "something else." Because I wasn't entirely sure—it had been hard to see in the fading light, after all—I spoke uncertainly. "I think there was mud on his jacket, near the shoulders. It looked like paw prints."

Miles frowned, no doubt remembering, as I was, the way Cisco had jumped up on the female park ranger yesterday, and how she had tried to brush the paw prints off her jacket. I could tell Miles was just trying to reassure the others when he said, "I'm sure Steele has everything under control."

I wanted to believe that. I was probably wrong, anyway. I had worn a forest service uniform, and I knew they didn't stay clean for long. There wasn't enough light to be sure it even *was* mud on his jacket. Name tags were easy to lose. And if he had seen Steele, Steele would have seen him. The whole thing was probably exactly what it appeared to be: an off-duty ranger stopping to check on us. Steele had everything under control.

BJ said, "I don't mind telling you, it's a relief to know Mr. Steele actually *is* close by. Maybe I won't sue him after all."

Reed looked at me skeptically. "How'd you know he was out of uniform?"

Before I could answer, Miles supplied, "Raine worked for the forest service."

"Oh, yeah?" Reed looked at me with new respect. "You were a forest ranger?"

"No kidding?" Max said. "That's interesting. Why'd you quit?"

So being a forest ranger was somehow more prestigious than being a dog trainer? And a wilderness search and rescue volunteer? I seriously did not think I'd ever understand these people's values. I replied simply, "Lack of funding." And they all nodded sympathetically.

Miles smiled. "Okay, I guess that was our excitement for the night. Theo, how about those mushrooms?"

Miles can make shoe leather taste good, and what he did with those mushrooms was nothing short of remarkable. He seasoned the mushrooms with crushed salted cashews, then snipped a couple of cans apart, pounded them flat with a rock, and used them to roast the chicken-of-the-woods over the glowing embers of the cooking fire. I've always thought it was the psychological effect of a hot meal that made campfire cooking taste so good—and certainly none of us would have come to any lasting harm for having missed one dinner—but this unexpected treat in the middle of nowhere was, quite frankly, one of the best meals I've ever had.

Afterwards, Parker passed around the bottles of vodka and everyone indulged in a splash or two in their cans of water. Spirits were mellow as we sat on our rolled-up sleeping bags around the campfire, orange and yellow shadows dancing around us. After a while, I stopped worrying about the peculiar visit from the park ranger, and I noticed even Miles stopped casting concerned looks down the dark trail. Cisco lay at my feet, eyes half-closed with the warmth of the fire, panting gently in contentment.

Max, watching Cisco, said, "He really is a good dog, isn't he? If it was my bichon out here, he'd be barking himself hoarse every time a squirrel jumped off a branch."

"Cisco's used to the outdoors," I said. "He knows what's important to bark at."

Reed said, "You know, I hate to admit it, but this isn't half bad. It's been a long time since I sat around a fire doing nothing."

BJ agreed, "It's not as bad as I expected. And hey, we did a good job setting up this camp, didn't we?"

"You did a great job," I said. "I say you all get As for today's work."

"Of course," Parker put in, "if we're completely honest, Steele made it easy on us. Not," he added quickly, holding up a defensive hand at the indignant protests that began, "that there was anything easy about hauling four hundred pounds of rock up from the creek or strapping tree branches together to build a house. But, come on. He picked this place where everything we needed was within a couple of hundred yards—firewood, windbreak, moss for insulation, water, and even food. All we had to do was put in a little effort and here we sit with all the comforts of home."

There were a few scoffing laughs, and Theo said, "How much vodka did you put in your water, anyway?"

"All I'm saying is, this is a Boy Scout camp compared to some of the situations Miles and I have been in," Parker replied. He glanced at Miles. "Am I right?"

I glanced at Miles, but his face, planed in the light of the fire, was unreadable. I would have very much liked to hear about some of those situations, but I had a feeling that was one of those things Miles preferred not to talk to me—or anyone—about.

Miles poked at the fire with a green stick, sending sparks showering into the air. "All we need is a bag of marshmallows," he agreed, "and it would be just like camp."

"I was in the Girl Scouts," Max said, "believe it or not. I hated it."

"That I believe," BJ said.

"We learned to make brownies over an open fire," added Max. "They tasted like charcoal."

Everybody chuckled.

Then Miles said, "Seriously, guys. I'm proud of you." His eyes moved around the half-circle, resting on each of his team members in turn. "I know, and you know, that if you were to find yourself in a real emergency, God forbid, it would be nothing like this. You *would* look back on all this and it would seem like a week at a spa in comparison. What I hope today has given you is a little bit of self-reliance, and the confidence that you can handle other things, harder things, that come your way."

There was a somber silence as everyone absorbed

and appreciated this. Then Miles added, "But do me a favor, okay? Don't get yourselves into any situation worse than this."

Everyone laughed, breaking the tension, and Ian said, "Well, I think it's important to acknowledge that none of this would have been possible without our intrepid leader." He raised his can of water to me. "Well done, Miss Stockton."

To my surprise, this was followed by a chorus of "Hear, hear!" and raised cans. I felt my cheeks flush in the darkness, and Miles grinned, squeezing my shoulders and kissing my cheek. "I knew I chose the right survival tool."

I pushed at his chest playfully.

We sat for a little while longer, building up the fire and chatting in an easy, unstrained way, and once again I was struck by how hard it was to believe that any of these people were guilty of what one of them had surely done, and how much I hoped none of it was true. Then Miles said, "We should probably get some rest. It's supposed to storm tomorrow, and we want to be out of here before it moves in."

"Don't let the fire die down," I added, standing to unroll my sleeping bag. Cisco stood, too, yawning widely and stretching out his forepaws. BJ reached forward to scratch his chin and he happily trotted over to her. "You'll probably wake up several times during the night, so when you do, add a log to the fire. And," I added, addressing the ladies in particular, "if you leave the camp for any reason, be sure to keep your eyes on the fire and walk straight back toward it to return. All you have to do is turn half a degree and you can become completely disoriented in the woods at night."

"Don't you worry about that," Max assured me, "when I get up to pee, it will be right over there." She pointed to a clump of scraggly cedars about six feet away. "So everybody else can just mind your own business."

This made everyone chuckle again, and there were some good-natured jokes back and forth between the men and the women. The creepy park ranger was forgotten. Even Steele, looking down on us with his binoculars, was far to the back of our minds. We were almost comfortable.

And somewhere deep in the woods the buzzards, having found their prey, feasted.

CHAPTER TWENTY-EIGHT

Miles and I took the smallest shelter and, zipped in our separate sleeping bags with Cisco between us for warmth, we couldn't have been toastier. Everyone slept restlessly. Cisco started whenever somebody got up to add a log to the fire, which Miles did several times, and once he woke me with a low growl. I had been dreaming about riding in the back of my father's vintage Chevy pickup truck, bouncing over a sun-drenched dirt road with Cisco on one side of me and Casey on the other, the engine roaring in my ears. My father had died and the truck had been sold long before Cisco was born and before I even knew Casey existed, which was the magic of dreams. I was anxious to get back to it, so I simply draped a soothing hand over Cisco's neck and sank back into sleep again.

Before I knew it, the pickup had turned into a sled,

and I was being pelted by snowflakes that felt like pebbles. Miles shook me awake. "Wake up, sugar," he said. "The rain is moving in early. We need to head out."

I sat up groggily and felt something cold plop onto my hair from the branches overhead. Rain. So much for our weatherproof shelter.

The scene outside was like something from an apocalyptic movie. A murky fog rose from the ground and mingled with the cloud of smoke from an almost extinguished campfire. A couple of my fellow campers moved through the gray curtain of mist like zombies, stiff and silent. Everything was black-and-white, one-dimensional. I wished I was back in that sunny pickup truck with Cisco and Casey.

I snapped on Cisco's leash and took him across the trail to the creek bank, where he lifted his leg on several bushes. I made use of the improvised ladies' room and splashed a handful of icy creek water on my face. According to my watch, the current temperature was 39 degrees. We definitely needed to get moving. The rain was barely a drizzle now, but it was forecast to get worse. The short walk to Steele's vehicle would be miserable enough even now.

When I returned, I could tell immediately something was wrong. Miles and Parker were talking earnestly to Theo. BJ and Max, puffy-faced and red-eyed, looked lost. Reed, coming up the trail at a determined pace, called out worriedly. "Nothing."

Before I could ask, Miles told me, "Ian is missing."

"His shelter is next to mine," Theo explained. He

rubbed his hands together nervously. "I heard him get up sometime during the night to put wood on the fire but didn't hear him come back again. I don't know how long ago that was."

I felt my chest tighten with alarm as I glanced around the group. I knew I wasn't the only one who was thinking about the strange visit from the park ranger last night. "Did anyone else see him after we went to bed?"

"Most of us were up a couple of times during the night," Parker said, "tending the fire. I can't say I noticed who was here and who wasn't at any given time though."

Miles's gaze seemed fixed on Theo with an odd intensity, but he let me do the talking. I peered through the murky gray light anxiously. "Did you check the woods?"

"As best we could," Miles said, finally glancing at me. "About fifteen- or twenty-feet in."

"I walked down the trail to where it starts to curve," Reed said. "Didn't see anything. I don't see how he could've gone farther than that in the dark without a flashlight. Or why he would."

It occurred to me that we didn't know whether or not he'd had a flashlight. He hadn't carried a pack, but he wasn't participating in the exercise and Steele hadn't checked his pockets. Because it didn't hurt to try, I called loudly, "Ian! Call out if you can hear me!"

We all waited in tense silence but heard nothing but the plop and sizzle of rain on the dying embers of the fire.

"When did the rain start?" I asked.

Parker replied, "Maybe twenty minutes ago."

Contrary to popular belief, tracking dogs actually pick up scents better in wet weather, although if it had been raining all night, I might have been a little more worried about Cisco's ability to focus on the exact direction in which Ian had left camp. This cool dampness, though, should have held the scent particles perfectly.

"Cisco should be able to pick up his trail," I told Miles. "You'd better get everyone else to Steele and let him know what happened. He has a vehicle waiting at the end of the trail, about twenty yards east on the service road."

BJ's voice was torn between reluctance and anxiety. "But shouldn't we help search?"

I shook my head. "Better if we go alone. Too many people only confuse the trail."

Reed said hopefully, "Wait. Is this part of the class? The insurance guy hides in the woods, and you show us how your dog can find him?" He looked around the group. "I mean, why else would she have brought her dog?"

"Afraid not," I replied quickly, before anyone else could latch on to the idea. "As far as I know, this is the real thing."

Although I had to admit, the whole thing was suspicious. Steele had given me such a hard time about even bringing my dog, and now Ian, the only member of the group who wasn't participating in the class, had disappeared. Had Steele recruited him as part of some lesson? Or perhaps to set me up for failure?

It was a hopeful notion, but not a very convincing one. Ian had not struck me as someone who would endanger his campmates by participating in a hoax like that and neither, to be fair, would Steele. Any of us could become lost or injured looking for a missing teammate who wasn't really missing, and Steele, as much as I disliked him, had better sense than to set something up like that. Besides, even if it was part of some stupid survival exercise, I had to treat each and every search like a legitimate rescue. There was always a chance that it actually was.

While the others doused the remnants of the fire and rolled up their sleeping bags, I snapped on Cisco's tracking leash and let him sniff Ian's sleeping bag. He was delighted to be back on the job when I gave him the signal to track, scenting the ground with enthusiasm and then bounding off to explore the track. He circled the camp a few times, sifting scents, while everyone else looked on curiously. Then, to my surprise, Cisco turned, nose to the ground, not toward the woods but toward the trail. I expected him to veer off into the woods and I moved quickly to keep up, but Cisco plotted a determined course straight up the trail, following the path we'd taken last night when we'd discovered Steele's camp.

Cisco is a good tracking dog and for the most part completely accurate, but he does have a tendency to get distracted. I was worried he might be following the track we ourselves had laid the evening before, or that he'd picked up on Steele's trail as he made his way to the road. But it was just as likely that Ian, having woken up earlier than everyone else, had followed this logical path north toward the place Steele had arranged our rendezvous. As a handler, it was not my job to try to outthink my dog. I just had to follow where he led.

The rest of the group couldn't contain their curiosity, and I suspected some of them agreed with Reed: this must be just another exercise they were supposed to observe. They shouldered their sleeping bags and followed us up the road, although I heard Miles telling them to stay quiet and stay back. He needn't have worried. Cisco was intrepid, weaving from side to side as he drank up the scent, occasionally doubling back to half the length of the leash to double-check his work and then leaping forward again, never breaking stride. He knew exactly where he was going.

We reached the dirt road and the tension in my chest relaxed when Cisco, still tracking, turned in the direction that Steele's Navigator had been parked last night. Of course. Ian had simply left camp earlier this morning, followed the trail to the road, and met Steele at the vehicle, where they both were no doubt now waiting for us.

The black Navigator crouched on the side of the road like a metal monster in a sci-fi movie, half covered in cold, swirling fog. Beyond it, atop the ridge, I could just make out the scrap of blue tarp that indicated Steele's campsite. Somewhat to my surprise,

Cisco stopped short of the vehicle and veered off the side of the road, nose still to the ground, just before he reached it. He was ten feet ahead of me, at the end of the leash, and obscured by the shadow of the vehicle, when I heard his single, sharp alert bark. He had found something.

I quickened my pace, calling, "Ian?" when I saw Cisco sitting by the side of a gully opposite the car. As I drew closer, I saw a shape in the ground fog, a man collapsed in the weeds by the side of the road. I ran.

Ian was lying face-down in the dried grass, perfectly still. The rain had soaked the back of his jacket and liquified the dark stain there into a steady stream of diluted blood that dripped into the mud. I dropped to my knees and felt for a pulse with cold, shaking fingers. I grasped his shoulder. I knew before I turned him over that he was dead. Sightless eyes stared up at me and the sharp point of a metal projectile protruded from his chest.

CHAPTER TWENTY-NINE

I don't know how long I knelt there, my heart pounding, my breath a lump in my throat. It felt like hours but was probably less than a minute. The others weren't far behind me. I got to my feet on watery legs and called hoarsely, "Here!"

By the time Miles and Parker jogged up, with the others only a few steps behind, I had regained my senses enough to release Cisco and pull his reward toy from his pack. It often seems bizarre to engage a dog in play after a gruesome find such as this, but without that immediate shift of emotions, the dog will shut down and lose his motivation to ever work again. Why wouldn't he? I felt like shutting down myself.

Miles looked at the man on the ground, and then at me. Whatever he might have asked was answered in my eyes. Parker stripped off one glove and knelt beside Ian, feeling for a pulse as I had done. He shook his head. "Skin is still pliable," he said, standing. "He's only been dead a couple of hours."

I heard BJ, arriving just as Parker stood to reveal the body on the ground, gasp, "Oh my God!" Max stifled a small scream as she, too, took in the truth of the matter. Reed said, "Jesus Christ, is he…"

And suddenly Miles spun around and grabbed Theo by the front of his jacket, demanding hoarsely, "What did you *do*? What the *hell* did you do?"

There followed a blur of chaos so quick and intense I really didn't comprehend it until it was over. Theo tried to wrestle out of Miles's grip. Somebody screamed. Parker grabbed one of Miles's arms. I dropped Cisco's toy and grabbed Miles's other arm, trying to pull him away. Parker shouted, "Let him go, man!"

It was only when Miles stepped back, eyes churning and chest heaving, that the spinning pieces in my head started to come together into a partial picture. Theo put a shaking hand to his throat, rubbing the red mark that was left by his jacket when Miles pulled it tight. Reed and BJ and Max looked from the lifeless body on the ground to Miles and the growing horror on their faces was matched only by their confusion. I said uncertainly, "It was Theo? Theo stole the code?"

Theo shot a look at me, and I saw by the alarm there that I was right. Miles never took his eyes off Theo. He said coldly, "There was a tracker embedded in the code. I've been watching you since you got here. You left camp this morning at 5:00 a.m., three minutes after Ian did. When you returned, the code wasn't with you. I'm going to ask you one more time. *What did you do?*"

BJ whispered, "Oh, my God."

Parker's brows drew together. "The Salus project. We thought so."

Max pressed her fingers to her lips, her glance flickering to the body on the ground. "This can't be happening."

And Reed glared at Theo. "You stupid son of a bitch."

For half a moment, Miles's glance darted around the group, and he looked almost surprised. "You knew?"

"Oh, for God's sake, Miles," BJ said shakily. "We wouldn't be smart enough to work for you if we weren't smart enough to figure out what was really going on here. We were just waiting for you to tell us."

Theo took a half step back. His lips were white, and he was trembling visibly. "Look, I don't ... I don't know what you're talking about. This man is—is dead and..."

"And you killed him," Miles said harshly. "Who was he, Theo? And what did he do to deserve this?"

"You're crazy!" Theo cried. He took another step back, looking wildly around as though for support from the group—or, failing that, escape. "You're talking like... this man is dead, and we have to... you're crazy!"

Reed and Parker moved closer to Theo, pinning him in a circle facing Miles. Because I could see no one else was going to do it, I put on my other glove and knelt beside Ian's body. This was not the first dead body I'd touched, but it never got easier. My stomach curled as I searched his pockets, gloved fingers brushing lifeless flesh, until I found the phone. I stood up and handed it to Miles.

Miles held the phone up to Theo. "Is this yours?"

He shook his head. "Of course not."

"You're the only one who brought a phone," Reed said harshly. "How long have you been planning this?"

Miles held up the phone screen to Theo's face. Theo tried to turn away, but Parker grabbed the back of his hooded jacket at the neck and held him steady. Facial recognition unlocked the phone. The screensaver was a picture of Theo and his wife. He held it up for the others to see.

"All right!" Theo spat, jerking away from Parker. "All right, it's my phone! That doesn't prove anything!"

"According to the tracker," Miles said, "it proves the software is here. It proves you left camp at dawn to meet Ian and give him this phone with the Salus code on it. So I ask you again, who was Ian? What was your deal?"

Theo looked around, sucking air through his flared nostrils, trapped and on the verge of panic. He saw no friendly faces, no friendly eyes meeting his own. "All right." He breathed out a desperate puff of frosty air. "All right, I downloaded the source code. Why shouldn't I? It was mine! I designed the damn thing. Without me, it wouldn't exist. I deserved to be paid for it."

"You were paid," Miles said, working hard to keep his voice even, "almost a million a year while you were developing the code, and a handsome bonus when I bought the company and brought you over to supervise the project."

"It was my intellectual property," he insisted. "I had a right!"

"Who was Ian?" Miles demanded again.

Theo turned his eyes deliberately away from the body on the ground. "A broker. I don't know his real name or who he worked for. He arranged this whole thing. To meet here, to exchange cryptocurrency for the source code. I don't know what he was going to do with it afterward."

"Sell it to the damn Russians!" Reed said furiously. "Or the Chinese! You stupid maggot, what the hell were you thinking?"

And BJ said bitterly, "You poor idiot. I hope he paid you enough to make your life in prison comfortable."

Miles didn't take his eyes off Theo. "Did you find out the code was a trap? Is that why you killed Ian—before he could discover it for himself and come after you?"

The last of the color drained from Theo's face. I literally had never seen a man so bloodless... alive. "What... what do you mean, a trap? What are you talking about?"

"Let me take a guess on this one," Reed said, still glaring at Theo. "You were set up. What you downloaded was worthless."

BJ added contemptuously, "Seriously, who did you think you were dealing with? The best cybersecurity team in the country has been working on these breaches for months."

Parker said, "So this"—he made a short, brutal gesture toward the body on the ground—"was for nothing."

"I didn't kill him," Theo said hoarsely. "How could I? I don't have any weapons. You know that! You saw what I brought with me! He was alive when I walked away from here," he rushed on. "We made the exchange, he was going to use Steele's car to get away... he had a device that cloned Steele's key fob, it was all part of his plan... but I was worried about being seen so I left him here... the last I saw he was walking toward the car. He was alive!"

I felt a prickle of cold on the back of my neck that wasn't rain, and I looked back toward the splash of blue on the ridge. Surely Steele would have seen or heard what was going on down here by now. Where was he?

Miles demanded, "Was Steele in on this?"

Theo shook his head adamantly. "No. Not that I know of anyway. I only had contact with Ian. You've got to believe me. I didn't kill him!"

After a moment, Parker said quietly, "Miles, that's a crossbow bolt in Ian's chest. It had to be fired by somebody who knew what he was doing."

Theo said desperately, "I don't have a crossbow! I don't even know what one is!"

Miles looked at the body. He looked at me. We were

both remembering the blood we'd seen in the gully by the trail, and the hunter.

Miles said, "The police can straighten this out. We need to get back to civilization and notify them. Who has rope?"

I stripped the paracord loop off my wrist and handed it to him. "Steele has a sat phone," I reminded him. "I'll check out his shelter."

Miles grabbed Theo's wrists and twisted them behind his back. Theo fought him, crying, "Hey, you can't do that! I told you, I didn't…"

Reed looked disturbed. "Where is Steele, anyway? You don't suppose… could he have caught Ian trying to steal his car and…"

"Yes, that must be it!" Theo struggled against Miles's restraint. "It was Steele!"

"Shut up or I swear I'll punch you out," Miles said. His voice was low and calm, the only sign of emotion a slight tightness that came from exertion as he wrapped Theo's wrists with the paracord and tied it off. But there was worry in his eyes when he looked at me. "I'll come with you."

Parker said, "I'd better come too. Reed, can you handle this sack of garbage?"

Reed replied grimly, "I've handled worse."

Miles looked around once more, scanning the road and the woods beyond. "Don't stand here in the open," he advised the rest of the group. "Get off the road. See if you can get into Steele's car. But," he added, "don't set off the alarm. Not yet."

I pulled up the hood of my jacket against the

increasingly thick drizzle and we set off through the woods in the direction of the shelter. Parker said quietly, "Something's not right. Steele should have been here by now. Do you think Theo was telling the truth?

"About him not being involved?" Miles replied. "I don't know. But if it was a crossbow that killed Ian, I don't think Theo pulled the trigger."

"Did Steele have a crossbow?"

Miles didn't answer. The two men were behind me, so I didn't participate in the conversation. I didn't think it mattered anyway. The only thing that mattered was getting out of here. Steele had the only way to communicate with the outside world, and the keys to our only mode of transportation.

I let Cisco choose the path because it's true that an animal will always find the most direct route between Point A and Point B. Most major highways today started as game trails because several hundred years ago some deer discovered the fastest way to cross a mountain or reach a watering hole and wore a trail through the forest with its travels. Cisco might not know, in this case, precisely where we were going, but he could be counted upon to find the easiest way through the forest undergrowth.

Of course, it's also true that animals have four legs, and what seems like an easy path to them might not be the same to their human counterparts. We had only gone a few dozen feet when something caught Cisco's attention at the bottom of a rain-slick hill, and he scrambled toward it. I had no choice but to follow, completing most of the distance sliding on my butt.

"You okay?" Miles called.

I raised an arm in reassurance. "Fine!" I got to my feet, and as I did, I saw what had caught Cisco's interest. I felt my blood freeze. A few feet away Cisco was pawing at the dirt and rotted leaves to reveal what was buried there. It was a human arm.

CHAPTER THIRTY

I cried hoarsely, "Cisco, leave!" and pulled backward on the leash so hard that I fell down again. Cisco immediately came and sat beside me, looking anxious and uncertain. I couldn't make my eyes stop staring at the horror before me.

The arm was not connected to a body. It was streaked with mud and dirt and defined at the shoulder by torn bloody tendons that had already begun to rot. The tips of the fingers were capped by nails painted bright pink.

Behind me, Parker said, "Shit."

And Miles whispered on a single stunned breath, "Christ."

I wrapped an arm around Cisco's neck, mostly for support. My whole body was quaking. "The... ranger," I managed.

Parker moved carefully around, searching, his boots making soft scuffling sounds on the wet leaves. Miles took my shoulders and lifted me gently to my feet. "Okay?" he said.

I gulped and nodded. I wasn't okay. Who would be? Two days ago this woman had been laughing and petting Cisco. Now she was dead. Someone had killed her and cut her body into pieces and scattered those pieces in the woods. No, I wasn't okay.

"The park ranger," I said, forcing my voice steady through chattering teeth. "Her nails... they were bright pink. It's her." It was important to say that. She was a person. She had been alive. Now she wasn't. It was important. "She was..." My voice fell to a broken whisper. "She was leaving on vacation." The vacation she would never see. The plans she would never fulfill. I couldn't stop shaking.

Miles's arm was firm and steady around my shoulders. He said nothing, which was the best thing he could do.

Parker returned to us, his face sallow and damp, his fist pressed just below his nostrils. "There are more remains over there," he said, jerking his head toward the direction from which he'd come. His voice was tight and strained. "I couldn't tell... maybe a foot, part of a leg. There've been carrion eaters."

I took a breath, trying to steady myself. Cisco pressed close to me, his anxious panting in counterpoint to the plop of raindrops from the branches overhead.

Miles looked around wordlessly, found a stick, and planted it close to the first find. "Does anybody have a handkerchief or something?"

I dug into Cisco's backpack for the empty cellophane bag from the dehydrated dog food that had been his dinner last night. It was bright orange. Miles pushed it onto the stick like a flag. "Let's go," he said, his expression grim.

We started up the hill toward the shelter. Less than fifty feet later we found Steele's body splayed out face-down behind a thick fallen tree trunk. It was easy to see, by the disturbed forest floor and the damp blood trail, that he had been dragged there. A metal arrow, like the one that had felled Ian, protruded from the back of his neck.

Cisco, who had traveled in front of us with his nose to the ground, had been the one to alert us to the bloody patch of earth a few feet away from the fallen tree. By that time I think we were all in such a state of shock that finding the body seemed like a simple inevitability. We all remained motionless for what seemed like the longest moment, staring down at the body mutely. For some reason, I couldn't get the image of Wild Bill Hickok out of my mind, sprawled face-down with a bullet in the back of his head, holding the winning hand. I squeezed my eyes shut briefly, trying to blot out the picture. Trying to focus.

Miles stepped over the fallen log and knelt beside Steele. He pressed his hand briefly to the side of Steele's neck and shook his head, not looking up.

"Jesus," breathed Parker. "It's a damn killing field."

Miles looked around, scanning the forest for whatever danger might still be lurking there. "Rigor has started to set in," he said. "This probably happened sometime last night. Maybe even yesterday afternoon."

I felt sick, remembering how Cisco and I had passed by these very woods on the trail to the road yesterday. Had Steele been dead then? Had his killer been watching us?

Cisco, sensing my distress, pressed close to me, tail wagging low. I wanted to stroke him, reassure him with my voice, but my hands were trembling too badly, and I didn't trust my voice.

Miles started going through Steele's pockets. Parker saw the gun on the ground and picked it up. He opened the magazine, checked the ammunition, and told us, "Loaded." I guess that was supposed to make us feel better.

Parker zipped the gun into his jacket pocket and added, "His knife is gone."

Miles stood up. "No keys, no wallet, no cell phone."

Parker said quietly, "I don't think Theo had anything to do with this, boss."

Miles looked back toward the trail, his face tight, eyes narrowed. "You two go back to the car. I'll get the sat phone from the shelter."

"No," Parker and I said at once. Parker added firmly, "We stay together."

There was only the quickest flash of debate in Miles's eyes, but he had to see the logic of it. He had to also see that neither Parker nor I was leaving without him. "Yeah, okay," he said. "Let's go."

We scrambled up the hill with Cisco leading the way. I was barely aware of Parker and Miles beside me until we reached Steele's shelter. His campfire still smoldered with a few damp gray sticks, but it was clear no one had tended it in hours. The blue tarp, stretched between two trees and insulated in the back with spruce boughs, protected an open sleeping bag and the day pack positioned to be used as a pillow. The last moments of a man's life, caught in a silent tableau. Nothing appeared to have been disturbed. It all looked as though he had just stepped away for a moment and might be back at any second to discover us rifling through his things.

The two men searched around the outside of the shelter for the sat phone. I knelt and unfastened his pack. Flashlight, paracord, matches, and other camping necessities. No med kit. Worse, no satellite phone. I picked up the sleeping bag and looked in the corners of the shelter. Cisco sniffed around but found nothing more than I had.

"It's gone," I said aloud, sitting back on my heels. "The phone is gone."

Miles said grimly, "No, it's not."

He was holding several pieces of broken black plastic in his hands. The shattered remnants of the satellite phone.

Parker blew out a long, slow, frosted breath. His expression was bleak. "Well," he said. "I guess help really isn't coming."

Miles tossed the crushed pieces of useless technology aside and started untying the tarp. After a moment Parker and I moved around to the other side to help him. Nobody needed to ask why he wanted the tarp. We knew.

I shouldered Steele's pack, and we went back down

the hill. We covered Steele's body with half the tarp and took the other piece back to the road, where the others stood huddled near the car. Miles waited until he had covered Ian's body with the remaining tarp to tell them, as succinctly as possible, what we had found. For a moment, everyone was too shocked to speak. I heard Max stifle a sob. "Good God, what *is* this?"

BJ put an arm around Max's waist. Her face was hollow-eyed and haggard, and her voice choked. "Did I," she managed, "did I hear you say… body parts?"

The temperature was dropping steadily, and the cold drizzle had turned into a light rain, with occasional gusts of wind driving needlepoints into our skin. Weatherproof coats glistened damply, and water dripped from the hoods. My hair, where it escaped from my hood, was plastered to my forehead. So was BJ's and Max's. Yet none of us, in that moment, seemed to be aware of our physical misery. The horror of it was all too big.

Parker said, "Something is going on here that has nothing to do with us."

Theo cried, "I told you! I told you it wasn't me!" He sat on the wet ground with his hands tied behind his back where, apparently, Reed had put him. His hood had come off and his face and hair were soaked. "Untie me! I had nothing to do with…"

Reed said coldly, "Shut up." No one else even looked at Theo.

BJ said desperately, "But—what about the phone? The satellite phone? Didn't you say…"

Miles shook his head. "It's gone."

I found my voice abruptly. "We have to get back to the radio at the lodge. We can call the ranger station from there."

Reed said, "The car is locked. We found this..." He held up a small device, not much bigger than a key fob, to Miles. "Down the hill there, in a ditch. I guess it fell when Ian..." His jaw tightened, but he didn't seem able to finish the sentence. Instead, he went on, "It must've been sitting in the water for a couple of hours. It doesn't work."

Miles nodded. "Okay then. We walk."

"But..." Max looked helplessly at me. "Five miles? Didn't you say last night it was five miles to the lodge?"

"By the road," I agreed. "The trail is half that distance. Leave the sleeping bags here, and anything else you can't carry in your pockets. We'll be back at the lodge in less than an hour."

"The road is too open," Miles said, confirming my decision. His eyes kept scanning, scanning the woods around us. "We go back the way we came."

BJ looked at the body on the ground, her eyes filling with distress. "Do you mean... leave him here?"

"We have to," Miles said grimly. "No choice. Let's go." And without another word, he turned and led the way back toward the trail.

CHAPTER THIRTY-ONE

Mistakes happen. Accidents happen. Failures happen, even to the best of hunters. Once Jessup had stepped over a rattlesnake in the process of striking; the damn thing had missed and struck his boot. A mistake for the rattlesnake, because Jessup had blown it apart with a .44 about five seconds later. Another time he had watched a mountain lion, one of the most perfect predators in the wild, spring for a rabbit only to watch it slip right through his paws. Jessup doubted the mountain lion spent much time brooding over its failure. Shit happens. Do better next time.

Jessup's encounter with the rich tourist campers had given him an idea, and a plan began to form. Retirees with checking accounts were one thing; you could get maybe four or five hundred a day before the bank flagged the account. But corporate cards were virtually unlimited. One hit could bring in fifteen or twenty thousand. And all he needed was one.

This was an entirely new game, slick and elevated. High stakes, low risk. The thought of it excited him. The best part was that the leader, the only one who knew what he was doing, had already been taken care of. All Jessup had to do was separate one from the pack and take him down. It didn't even matter which one, although he couldn't help hoping it was one of the women. By the time the others realized their companion was missing Jessup would have him—or her—bound and gagged and on the way to purgatory. By the time the authorities were notified, his victim would be well disposed of and Jessup several thousand dollars richer.

But sometimes the wind shifted. Sometimes a misstep, sometimes an unexpected turn, and the arrow, instead of striking a shoulder in a painful and debilitating wound, pierced the heart. Dead prey was useless prey in this particular case. Jessup needed ATM passcodes. Without them, the cards were just worthless pieces of plastic. What a waste.

But shit happens.

He tried not to brood over it. He tried not to get furious with himself. His time in this wilderness was almost over, counting down to hours instead of days. The pansy-ass tourists at the campfire had seen his face. There were bodies to be discovered only footsteps away. Patterns were starting to form. Bad, all of it bad. He couldn't afford another mistake.

Of course, he still had the advantage over them.

Without their technology they were helpless. They didn't know these woods, and without their leader, they couldn't hope to survive. Jessup had another advantage as well, one that was perhaps the most important tool in a hunter's belt. He knew how to think like his prey, to predict its behavior, and ultimately, to outsmart it.

They would return to the lodge. Maybe they had a radio there, maybe not. Either way, it would make little difference. This rain would turn to ice before the day was done. Drones wouldn't fly. Neither would helicopters. Even park service jeeps would struggle to reach them before morning. They would be spooked. One of them, perhaps more, would try to leave. And he would be ready for them.

All he needed was one.

CHAPTER THIRTY-TWO

Cisco and I led the way for the first half of the trek, with Miles walking beside us when the trail was wide enough. Parker and Reed brought up the rear with Theo between them, stumbling along with hands bound. We were a solemn and miserable group, heads bowed beneath rain hoods, boots splashing in the mud, shoulders rounding as the temperature dropped. Even Cisco seemed to trudge, his coat sodden, his head lowered, canvas saddlebags weighed down by the rain. Conversation was sporadic, consisting mostly of "Sorry," when a disturbed branch splashed water on someone else's face or "Watch your step," in a slick spot.

I remembered the dream of Casey and Cisco and me in the back of the pickup truck. How I longed to be back there now. But it had been after that dream that

Cisco growled. He must have heard Ian leaving camp, or Theo returning. That was what had awakened Miles and alerted him to look at the tracker on his watch.

I said, "It was Ian who took Cisco out into the woods the first night, hoping he would get lost. He couldn't take a chance on a barking dog interrupting his mission."

Miles said bitterly, "He stole air. Nothing. Literally, nothing. Ones and zeroes that didn't even amount to an actual code. But two people are dead for it, maybe three. It's so damn stupid. *Stupid*," he repeated through gritted teeth.

I touched his arm. "None of this is your fault," I said quietly.

He gave a single, sharp shake of his head as though trying to clear it. "Baby," he said wearily. "I need a better job."

"You can always come work for me." I tried to smile, and he tried to smile back.

I said, "You must have suspected Theo all along. You bought the company—the one he and Reed came over from—for the tech."

He nodded. "I thought the chances were good it was one of them. What got past me, what I was too mad and stupid to see, was Ian."

"He fooled everyone," I said. It was small comfort.

The woods grew darker on either side of the trail as the sky gave way to the coming storm, and the tension that pulsed between us all grew thicker. Every time a twig snapped or a gust of wind whistled, I could feel my muscles tighten. Eventually, I had to say what everyone was thinking. But I said it quietly, just to Miles.

"Do you think he's still here? Watching us?"

"I don't know," he admitted. "I can't outthink an enemy I don't know or understand. But we've got to assume we're in danger. We've got to get to shelter."

He held out a hand to stop my forward motion. "Hold on. Trail narrows here."

We had reached that narrow ledge over the sheer drop-off. The ledge had been nerve-racking enough to traverse in dry, sunny weather; it would take all my attention to get everyone safely across today. Instinctively I reverted to trail-leader mode. I stopped and called back, "Okay, single file now. One person crosses at a time. Stay close to the wall. Take your time. It might be slippery."

I sent the ladies across first, then Reed, watching anxiously until they were all safely on the other side. Parker was next, but Theo balked. "I can't get across with my hands tied," he told Miles, eyeing the ledge uneasily. "I'll need my balance. You've got to untie me."

Miles said shortly, "You know something? I don't care."

I understood how Miles felt. None of us would be here, stranded in the wilderness with a trail of dead bodies behind us, had it not been for Theo and his reckless scheme for riches he did not deserve. But I also knew Miles would never forgive himself, and neither would I, if Theo didn't make it across the ledge.

"Miles," I said reasonably, "he's right. It's too dangerous to cross with his hands tied."

Impatience and resignation crossed his face. "Cut him loose then."

I unfastened Cisco's leash from the clip on my pants and took out my multitool. "You go," I told Miles. "I'll send Cisco when you're across, and then Theo."

Miles started across and I cut the rope from Theo's wrists. As soon as he was free, Theo shoved me hard and lunged forward, running across the ledge. Cisco barked. I cried, "Miles, look out!"

Miles turned and tried to grab Theo as he ran past him. There was a horrible split second when they wrestled on the precipice and then Theo, with the strength of a desperate man, tore away, shoving Miles backward. There was shouting from the other side. Theo kept running. Miles threw out one arm, trying to catch himself against the wall of the hillside. The earth began to crumble away beneath his foot at the edge of the trail. He flailed for balance. I saw him start to fall.

I screamed, "*Miles!*" and lurched forward.

But it was too late. He was gone.

CHAPTER THIRTY-THREE

For one single cold, attenuated eternity absolutely nothing happened. No one moved, no one breathed. The rain didn't fall, the wind didn't blow. My heart didn't beat. Even the screams that would eventually form in my head were silent. Then, like a powerful wave, reality came crashing into me, a cacophony of noise and terror. Cisco barking. People shouting. Someone's shrill, high scream. Was it mine?

I cried, "Cisco, down!" I was dimly aware of him dropping to his belly, whining and licking his lips anxiously.

I heard Parker shout, "Raine, stay there!" But it was too late. I had already flung myself face-down onto the ledge, spreading out my weight so as not to trigger another landslide. I had to know. I turned my head to look over the side.

Miles was about three feet below me, his hands entwined in the roots of a small, partially sheared-off tree, his face bloodied and smeared with mud, but alive. Alive. I instinctively stretched my arm over the edge toward him.

"No point," he gasped. "I've got no leverage."

I knew that. Miles worked out every day and was as fit as any man I've ever known. Had he not been, it's unlikely he would have been able to stop his fall by grabbing the tree roots. But even if he had been able to gain purchase on the hillside and push himself up with his feet, the minute he let go to grab my hand he would risk his balance and we'd both go over. I knew that. But I extended my hand anyway because I just couldn't help it.

There was a buzzing close to my ear, and when I cautiously turned my head toward the sound I saw that my watch was scrolling: *For emergency assistance, press side button three times.* There was a long down-the-rabbit-hole moment in which I wondered how the watch knew we were in an emergency situation, and then I realized it must have interpreted my flinging myself to the ground as a fall. I retrieved my opposite hand from the ledge and pressed the button three times instinctively, just as though I actually expected a helicopter to magically appear overhead with a rescue ladder. As though I could clap and give Tinkerbelle her wings. As though I could click my heels and be home. But the truth was, as Steele had so accurately put it and as I knew all too well, we were on our own. Help was not coming.

I was wearing Steele's backpack with a full coil of paracord inside, but I couldn't reach it from this position. I would have to go back to the other side, remove the backpack, and crawl back out onto the ledge again. I said, breathing hard, "Hold on. I'll be back with rope."

I started to inch back, dirt crumbling over the edge with my every move. From somewhere above me, Parker called urgently, "Don't move. The shelf is unstable."

I heard movement in the woods to my right and with my peripheral vision saw Parker's booted feet side-stepping down the slick hill until he was standing just above me. "Paracord?" His voice was choppy and out of breath.

The paracord bracelet I wore had mostly been used up on the shelters, and I'd given the rest to Miles to tie Theo's hands. "In the backpack," I replied. "Steele has a couple of hundred feet. Can you reach it?"

I felt him unzip the pack and fumble around with the contents until he found the rope. "I'll tie off," he said, "and toss a harness down to you." To Miles, he called, "How're you doing there, boss? Can you hold on a little longer?"

Miles glanced down at the sheer fall beneath him and replied grimly, "I can hold on the rest of my life."

And that was exactly what it felt like: a lifetime while I heard Parker moving around in the woods, while rain plopped on the canvas backpack and dripped down the back of my neck, while Cisco whined in almost perfect counterpoint to the muffled staccato of a woman's sobs somewhere in the distance. While my heart beat in my ears. While I held on to the sound of Miles's breathing, harsh and heavy, like it was a lifeline.

"Not much longer," I whispered, struggling to get the words out. "Just focus. Breathe in, breathe out."

He kept his eyes firmly fixed on the cliff face. The smallest wrong move, even a turn of the head, can cause you to lose your balance in a situation like this, which was something he knew as well as I did. He said, "I don't think the fall will kill me." Each sentence was punctuated by short, choppy breaths. "I'll break some bones. Pelvis. Maybe spine. Don't try to rappel down. You'll need an airlift. Get back to the lodge as fast as you can and call for help."

"Shut up," I said fiercely. My nose was dripping, and so were my eyes. My voice was thick and wet. "We've been in worse situations than this. Just shut up."

"My fingers are cramping," he said. His voice was tight and hard to understand. I could see the shaking of the muscles of his arms from here.

"Focus," I shouted at him. "Focus, damn it!"

A loop of rope landed in front of my face. "Secure yourself first," Parker instructed from above me. "Then I'll toss down the rescue harness."

"Okay," I gasped to Miles, scrambling for the rope. "Almost there."

I wriggled into the safety rope, trying to move as little as possible. Clumps of dirt broke away beneath me and pummeled Miles's hair.

"Got you," Parker said, and I felt the knot tighten

as he tugged on the rope. "You've got about ten feet of slack."

"That's enough," I said. "Pay it out a couple of feet at a time."

"Reed's here to help," he said as I grasped the second rescue harness he dropped in front of me. "Tell us when."

I checked the knots and double-checked them, then leaned over the edge, feeling the rope tighten with my weight. More of the ledge broke away.

"I'm coming for you," I told Miles. "You know how this works. Once you're in the harness, hold on to the rope with both hands. It's tied off to a tree uphill. Parker and Reed will pull you up. It's going to be hard, but you can do it."

"Baby," he said, breathing hard, "I sure hope you're as good as you say you are."

I secured the rescue harness around my neck and grasped my rope with both hands. "I'm better," I assured him, and I somehow managed a quick, false smile. I called up to Parker, "Go!" and slid off the ledge into the air.

As soon as I left the ledge, the terror I had felt watching Miles cling to life by his fingers vanished. I used my hands to guide my descent and pushed my feet against the wall to maintain my position. The drop was only a few feet, but it was like crawling vertically as I inched toward Miles. When I was just below his feet I called up to Parker, "Stand by!" and to Miles I said, breathing hard, "Don't look at me. We've got you now. Don't do anything 'til I tell you."

I slipped the stirrups of the harness over his legs as quickly as I could while balancing against the side of the cliff. One of his pants legs was soaked with blood, but I couldn't pause to examine the wound just then. I tightened the final loop beneath his arms and told Miles, "Okay. Got you. Hold on to the rope."

One by one, he released his hands from the tangled tree root and transferred them to the rope above his head. He swung away from the cliff face. He tried to use his legs for balance but cried out in pain when the wounded one struck the side of the mountain. "It's okay," I told him. "Let them do the work."

A tight grunt of assent was his only answer.

I called up, "Secure!" and slowly, laboriously, they began to haul Miles to the top.

I was too anxious to wait for assistance with my climb, and by the time Parker and Reed pulled Miles up the hill to safety, I had reached the ledge. As I pulled myself over, the last of the ledge fell away in a shower of mud beneath me. Had Parker not already tightened the rope, I would have gone over with it.

Every muscle in my body burned as I scrambled up the hill where Miles lay. My dragged-in breaths sounded like sobs. Reed and Parker were gasping with exertion as they pulled Miles farther up the wooded slope that was thick with slippery leaves and almost as steep as the drop below. Later, I would wonder how they had even managed to get leverage for the rescue from that angle. In the distance I could hear Max and BJ calling out in relief, asking what they could do, but their voices were a blur to me. My focus was on Miles, his face smeared with blood and mud, his lips ashen and pressed together in pain.

When we finally reached a relatively level spot, Reed and Parker sank back to catch their breaths and I collapsed face-down next to Miles, flinging my arm over his chest. He turned his head weakly toward me but could not lift his arms to return my embrace. I heard a rustling in the woods behind us and pushed myself up in alarm, only to see that Cisco had broken his down-stay and was climbing the slick hill toward us. He wriggled anxiously through the woods to me, nuzzling my face. Rather than reprimand him, I flung an arm around his neck, hugging him weakly, letting his coat absorb the tears that soaked my face. "Good dog," I whispered, for absolutely no reason at all. "Good dog."

Miles said with an effort, "You guys... can expect a bonus."

"I'll take it," replied Parker, still trying to regulate his breath.

"Where's..." Miles's voice caught on a hitch of pain, and I turned to him anxiously. "Theo?"

It was Reed who replied, "On his way to hell, if there's any justice." He added grimly, "Gone. Hope he stays that way."

I sat up, shrugging the rescue rope over my head and pulling Miles free from his. Parker got to his knees and took the ropes from me. He was still breathing hard as he told Miles, "You are one lucky son of bitch."

"Copy... that," replied Miles. His voice was tight and growing weaker.

I wiped the blood from Miles's scraped face with my gloved hand and turned to examine his leg. The gruesome gash that slashed his leg midway between knee and ankle had opened up blue-black muscle and jagged flesh. His boot was already dark with blood, and I could see bone protruding. A wave of weakness flashed through my stomach.

Maybe he read it on my face, or maybe he already knew. Miles said, "It's—bad, right?"

"Yeah, well." I scrambled out of the backpack and unzipped it clumsily. "I don't think superglue is going to fix this one."

I tore through the backpack, forgetting the med kit had already been taken. Parker, seeing the wound for himself, slid down the hill toward me. Reed said in a low, sick voice, "Oh, Christ."

Miles tried to lift his head to get a look at the wound, but Parker blocked his view. There's something about seeing your own body mangled that will always, always strip away your will, I don't care how strong-minded you are.

"How bad?" Miles insisted hoarsely.

The first thing you learn when working with dogs is to control your emotions. Animals can sense your emotions in an instant and respond to them viscerally. When they go high with emotion, you go low. I had trained myself, over the years, to do just that in a crisis. It's not enough to just sound calm. You have to actually *be* calm. It's harder than it sounds.

"Bad enough," I replied, avoiding his eyes as I stripped off my jacket. My heart was racing and my throat was dry. *Damn it, damn it...* There had been morphine in Steele's med kit, real bandages, splints... "Compound fracture," I told Miles matter-of-factly. There was no point in lying to him, but I didn't want to make matters worse by letting him see how scared I was. "We need to stop the bleeding and get you to a hospital."

"Nothing hard, then," Miles said, dragging in breaths. "That's good."

Parker said, "Can you reduce the fracture?"

I shook my head, tearing the packaging off the remaining tampons that we hadn't used to start the fires. "I might compress a nerve or cut off circulation. We just need to stabilize it and transport." I handed him the multitool from my other pocket. "Rip the lining out of my jacket and cut it into strips. Reed," I called as Cisco nuzzled my arm again. "Take Cisco to BJ. But first, give me the water bottles out of his pack. And his tracking lead."

Reed came down the hill sideways, slipping and sliding on the slick surface, and took Cisco's lead. He handed me the two bottles that I had filled with boiled water last night and Cisco's ten-foot cotton lead. He said, "Wouldn't it be faster if one of us went ahead and radioed for help?"

I thought for the first time in what seemed like hours about the body parts in the woods, the two dead men. Parker spoke before I could. "Bad idea," he said. "We stay together."

Reed tugged at Cisco's leash, but Cisco was reluctant to leave me. I said, sparing him a quick glance, "It's okay, bud. You're a good boy. Go."

One of the most important things you can teach a dog is to go with a stranger in an emergency. Cisco had been through lots of emergencies, and he understood when his job was over. He didn't want to go with Reed, but he did it. I turned my attention quickly back to Miles.

I did my best to flush out the wound with the boiled water. I could see Miles biting back a cry of pain. I thought again, with furious regret, of all the things that would have been in an emergency kit. Painkillers, antiseptics… it was my fault. I should never have let Steele take my day pack. *You are responsible for your own survival.* Wasn't that what Steele had said? How could I have left emergency supplies behind?

Parker silently twisted the cap off a bottle of vodka and passed it to me. "Last one," he said grimly, and I remembered how recklessly everyone had passed the bottles around last night by the campfire.

I held the bottle to Miles's lips. "Drink some of this," I said. "It'll help a little."

Miles took a swallow and coughed. "It's gonna take more than that, babe."

I poured the rest of the vodka over the wound and once again he bit back a scream. I cut a length from Cisco's lead and tied it around Miles's leg just above the wound as a temporary tourniquet. Then I cut the tampons in half and began to pack them into the wound. They became soaked with blood almost as soon as I placed them. I held up my bloody hand without looking around and Parker placed the strips of flannel from my jacket in it.

"Listen to me," Miles said in a moment, panting. "Reed is right. I can't make it. The rest of you go. Radio for help. Leave me here. I'll be okay until help gets here."

"Are you crazy?" I hissed. I wrapped a strip of flannel around his leg as tightly as I dared, trying to compress the wound. "Somebody is walking around these woods with a crossbow killing people. Or did you forget that?"

"Leave me"—Miles ground out the words through clenched teeth— "the gun. It won't be long."

Parker said harshly, "Shit, man, this is not a B-Western." Then he knelt down and added, more gently, "Hey. We don't leave the wounded behind. Right?"

I liked Parker more at that moment than I'd thought it was possible to like any man with a $400 haircut... besides Miles, of course. And after a moment, I saw some of the tight lines around Miles's eyes relax. He gave a small nod. "Right," he said.

I finished wrapping Miles's leg, securing the bandages with the remainder of Cisco's lead, and carefully released the tourniquet. When no blood gushed, I tied it again, but not quite as tightly this time. If I kept it on too long, he could lose his leg. I stood, wiping my bloody hands on my pants. Parker handed me my jacket.

"We need to be careful moving him," I said. I scanned the woods for materials we could use. Sleeping bags. Why had I told everyone to leave them behind? The temperature was dropping, and Miles was starting to go into shock. The improvised bandage wouldn't slow the bleeding for long. We couldn't afford to stay out here in the open with a killer stalking the woods, maybe watching us right now…

Stop.

Think. Observe. Plan. Mistakes happen. Do better next time.

I took some deep breaths. The rain clicked on the leaves as it fell and clung to the branches overhead. It was starting to turn to ice. I dropped to one knee beside Miles and spread my weatherproof jacket over his torso, adding a meager extra layer of warmth. "The rest of the trail is flat and wide," I told him. "We'll be back at the lodge in no time. We'll radio the forest service, and they'll get you to an ER and send the police to deal with Ian and, you know, Steele. Everything's going to be fine. Just do as you're told and don't give us any trouble, okay?"

He tried to smile, but the effort was clearly too much for him. His face was the color of old oatmeal. "Yes, Captain," he managed.

I stood, pulling the hood of the vest I wore over my head. "Travois," I told Parker. "It'll take some time to build, but we can do it if we work together."

Parker nodded. "Better get started then." He started up the hill to gather materials. "Reed! Ladies! Let's go!"

CHAPTER THIRTY-FOUR

We stripped branches and used the paracord to secure them into a crude sledge, all of us working side by side in grim, urgent silence. Later, I would be amazed at how well these people—who, up until yesterday, I wouldn't have assumed capable of making themselves a cup of tea without assistance—performed under stress. And even then, I would be ashamed of myself because why should I be surprised? They were Miles's top team, and no one rose to inspire that level of confidence by being stupid or incompetent. I had been judging them unfairly from the moment I arrived and, even worse, silently accusing them of judging me. The truth was none of us would have made it through this crisis without the others.

It took less than half an hour for us to put together the crude travois and get Miles positioned on it. "It's not going to be very comfortable," I told Miles, "I'm sorry."

"I was expecting something a little more top tier," he replied, grimacing as I carefully moved his bandaged leg onto the sled. Already spots of blood were starting to show through the flannel wrappings. "Leather seats, maybe." The effort it had cost him to make the weak joke was clearly too much and he let his head loll back on the ground, shivering.

"We could cut some of those spruce limbs to keep the rain off him," Max suggested anxiously. "Maybe keep him warmer, too."

"Good idea," I said.

Parker pulled off his jacket and covered Miles with it as BJ and Max started to strip branches off the nearby spruce. "Here, take mine, too," Reed said, handing me his jacket. I must have looked surprised because he frowned and shrugged, "We'll be walking. Easier to stay warm."

BJ and Max brought back enough branches to cover Miles, and I fashioned a series of loose straps out of paracord to keep him stable on the sledge. I removed my pack and bunched it carefully underneath the injured leg to keep it elevated. Deep grooves formed on either side of Miles's mouth as he tried to hide the pain, and I suspected by the shallowness of his breathing that he had a broken rib or two he didn't know about yet.

I told the others, "Okay, this is how this works. We'll go in twos, each person taking one of the poles of the sledge. We can move faster that way, and no one will get too tired before it's time for the next team to take over. Fifteen minutes at a time."

"I'll go first," Reed volunteered. He looked miserable and anxious standing there in the cold and damp, and I felt bad about how quick I had been to judge him before. He had been my least favorite of the group, but we wouldn't have gotten this far without him.

"I'll take the other side," Max said before I could offer to do so.

BJ said worriedly, "How long do you think it will take to get there? Are you sure one of us shouldn't run ahead and radio for help?"

"No," I said sharply. "We've been through that. We stay together."

To my surprise, Miles spoke up in my defense. "She's right," Miles said hoarsely. The effort he made to get the words out was visible. "We can't afford... to lose anybody else, not even... to so much as a skinned knee."

"Says the guy who gets the luxury ride home," BJ replied, forcing a smile.

"Yeah." Miles let his head sink back against the rough crossbar of the sledge, his eyes closing. "It's good to be king."

And that was the last thing he said.

We set out while the temperature dropped steadily and the rain started to turn to ice, clicking when it hit our jackets and coating the tree branches overhead. We were too worried to talk much. I thought about

Steele, lying dead beneath the blue tarp in the woods while a sheet of ice formed atop it. I'd been so irritated with him, so impatient and annoyed. But he'd gotten us this far. He'd taught us how to survive. Even those of us who knew the techniques, he had bullied into putting them to use. He'd made me think. He'd reminded me what I could do. Now he was dead.

I thought about Ian with a metal arrow protruding from his chest. I thought about a severed arm with pink nails. I thought about Theo, pushing past Miles and not looking back as Miles went over the cliff. Why were we here? What did any of this have to do with us? Ones and zeroes, Miles had said. All this for ones and zeroes. How very, very nonsensical it all was.

The muddy ground slowed us down some, as did the icy rain, but the primitive drag sled worked exactly as it was supposed to. Miles faded in and out of consciousness, and every time I checked on him his skin seemed colder and clammier, his eyes more unfocused. Cisco trudged along beside us, his head down, his coat sodden and frozen in places. All of us looked constantly over our shoulders, startling at imagined dangers, waiting to be struck down.

Reed tried to keep our spirits up with lame jokes like, "The next time I get an invite for one of these fun corporate retreats, I think I'll schedule dental surgery instead," and "Let's all do this again next year, okay?" I appreciated the effort, however far it fell from its goal.

We slogged along in silence for a while, and then Max tried. "You know what I miss most right now?" she said. "The smell of fresh laundry."

Parker picked up the game. "The taste of a dirty martini."

"A steam bath," said Reed.

BJ said, "The way my little girl smells when I tuck her into bed." There was a catch in her voice at the end, and she quickly forced a smile, looking at me. "What about you, Raine?"

All I could think of was that stupid card game, Miles and Casey and Melanie and me sitting around the table in front of the fireplace, golden retrievers and Australian shepherds everywhere, a house that smelled like wet dogs and woodsmoke and a hundred years of safety. It had all seemed so commonplace at the time, so annoyingly familiar and unimportant. But that was a million years ago, and I would give all I had ever owned to be back in that moment now.

"Home," I said simply. "I miss home."

We didn't talk anymore after that.

The lodge came into view while Reed and Max were carrying the sledge. Miles was still clinging to consciousness, but I knew it was only because of his sheer stubbornness. Ice had formed a sheet over the branches that covered him and had started to accumulate on the ground in slick patches. My feet were so cold—despite the wool socks and thermal hiking boots—that my toes were numb. So were my fingers. Nonetheless, I broke away from the others at a jog, stumbling and slipping a little, with Cisco gladly running at my side and Parker not far behind. I noticed as I passed that the door to the metal building hung open, squeaking on its hinges in the wind. Had it been that way when we left? I didn't know or care.

I slammed into the door of the lodge and twisted the knob, but it didn't budge. "Locked!" I gasped to Parker as he bounded up the steps behind me. Of course it would be. And Steele had had the only key... except no one had it now.

Parker turned and called to BJ, who was a few yards behind us, "Try the back door!"

BJ raised her hand in acknowledgment and hurried around the back.

Cisco, cold and hungry and trying to be of help, flung his forepaws against the door. I told him, "Off!" and he dropped his paws to the ground, shaking icy water from his coat. Parker checked the windows. I fumbled in the pocket of my jacket with stiff fingers for my multitool, extracted it, and opened the awl. BJ jogged around the corner of the building.

"Locked," she reported. "Should we break a window?"

"No," I called back. I thrust the awl into the lock —a simple twist bolt—lifted up on the door handle, turned the awl sharply, and the lock gave way. I turned the handle and the door opened.

Parker looked at me with muted admiration. "How'd you do that?"

"My brother is a criminal," I replied briefly, hurrying inside. A pale gray light filtered in through the windows, and even though the woodstove contained nothing but ash, the relief of being out of the freezing rain made the building feel almost warm.

"Get the fires started. I'll radio for help, but it might be some time before they can get here."

"They'd better hurry," BJ said, following us inside. "The roads will ice up before long."

I unclipped Cisco's leash and tore off my gloves, flexing my frozen fingers as I moved, half running, down the corridor to the radio room. The little room was windowless, and when I switched on the overhead light, I noticed none of the lights on the radio were on. Had Steele turned the radio off for some reason while we were gone?

I went to the radio, Cisco leaving wet prints on the floor as he padded beside me, and toggled the radio switch up and then down. Nothing happened. I twisted the frequency knob, grabbing the microphone at the same time. The cord came away from the unit, dangling frayed wires. It had been cut. Heart pounding, I grasped the radio and turned it around. The back panel had been completely smashed in; the inner workings crushed.

I remembered Ian and Theo, having forgotten their jackets, walking back to the lodge after everyone else had left for the trailhead. Of course they would make sure we couldn't call for help until Ian had made his escape. Of course.

I sat down heavily in the straight-backed chair in front of the radio table, the sound of my own breathing gushing in my ears. Cisco put his head on my knee, and I threaded my fingers through his cold, wet fur. I needed to find his towel and dry him off. I needed to get my first aid kit and find some pain medication for Miles. I needed to get us all out of here. But right then all I could do was sit and stare at the wrecked radio. And try to remember to breathe.

I heard voices in the other room, smelled the sulfur of a struck match and the wisp of smoke. *Okay*, I thought. *Okay.*

I stood and looked around the room. There wasn't much. A wall of steel shelves stocked with cardboard boxes, cleaning supplies, twelve-packs of toilet paper and paper towels. A canvas bag of tools. I knew the bag contained tools because the hammer that had no doubt been used to smash the radio lay on top. There was a cheap, two-drawer metal file cabinet next to the radio table. When I tried to open it, the top drawer was locked. This time I didn't bother with the lock-manipulation techniques Casey had taught me. I grabbed the hammer and inserted the claw beneath the lip of the drawer, wrenching it toward me. The metal bent but the lock did not give.

"What are you doing?"

I turned to see Parker at the door. "Ian and Theo smashed the radio," I said. "I think our phones are in this drawer. Give me a hand."

Parker looked in disbelief, and then anger, at the radio. He swore curtly and took the hammer from me, bracing his foot against the bottom drawer and using the hammer to pry open the top one. Metal screeched and the lock popped loose. The basket containing our phones was inside.

I took out the basket and retrieved my phone, with the colorful paw print case Melanie had given me for my birthday, and then Miles's. I passed the basket to Parker and started typing out a desperate text to 911 on my phone.

Parker said, "That won't…" And then he stopped, understanding. I pushed send and stood up. The phone would keep trying to send the message until it was successful, and long before I was able to make a call, I might come into a reception area just long enough for the message to get through.

Parker retrieved his own phone and led the way back to the keeping room. I unbuckled Cisco's saddlebags, grabbed my first aid kit from the bunk room, and followed him.

A fire was blazing in the woodstove and Miles, covered with a sleeping bag, was on the sofa in front of it. He was conscious, his nostrils flared with every breath, emphasizing the very real effort he made to remain functional as Reed carefully piled cushions under his foot to elevate his leg. BJ and Max were in the kitchen, making tea and heating up cans of soup.

I said, without preamble, "First, the radio is out. Ian and Theo probably smashed it before we left."

There was a stunned silence as everyone absorbed the news. Reed stared at me for a long moment before saying, "Well, now we're screwed."

BJ, hovering near the entrance to the kitchen, said, uncertainly, "But why would…" She broke off, no doubt realizing how foolish that sounded.

"Ian wanted to give himself a solid head start," Parker said. "Making sure we couldn't call the authorities when we made it back here." He put the basket with the phones on the table. "But here are your phones."

A gust of wind rattled the windows and pellets of rain and ice clattered steadily on the metal roof. I took a breath and went on, "Second, does anybody have anything stronger than ibuprofen? Anything at all. Now's not the time to be shy."

Max said hesitantly, "I've got some Ambien."

"Sold," Miles said tightly, holding out his hand to her.

"Okay," I said, "that'll help." Max hurried to the bunk room, and I retrieved the bottle of ibuprofen from my first aid kit, shaking out four tablets. "This should take the edge off," I told Miles, handing him the pills. "It won't be much longer."

BJ brought him a glass of water. "If the radio's out, I don't see how…"

"This fool woman is going to hike down the hill until she gets a cell phone signal," Miles interrupted gruffly. He slammed down the pills with a gulp of water. "In an ice storm."

"We don't have a choice," I returned sharply. "We have to report two deaths and a killer on the loose and"—I felt a catch in my throat as I finished— "get you to a hospital before sepsis sets in. The park service isn't supposed to check on us until Friday, and if we get iced in it could be longer."

"Didn't say you weren't right, sugar," Miles said. His voice was hoarse and a little choppy. "Just said you were crazy."

I literally felt the stiff muscles of my face melt into

a weary smile as I sank down onto one knee beside him. "Hey," I whispered. I caught his cold fingers in mine. "The only thing I'm crazy about is you, okay? One hundred percent."

He returned my smile weakly. "Good to know," he said, "since my life is pretty much in your hands."

I tightened my grip on his fingers and pressed them to my lips. My eyes burned with a sudden gush of unshed tears. "I love you," I whispered thickly. "I really do. And..." I retrieved my hand, swiped away the tears, and glanced around the room, trying for a lighter tone. "These people seem pretty devoted to you, God knows why. We're in a mess, but it's nothing we can't handle. So just try to relax and let us take care of it, okay?"

He leaned his head back against the arm of the sofa. "Think... I can do that," he agreed shakily.

I held out his phone to him. "Unlock this. And bring up the name of your friend in the FBI. I want to send him a text."

It took several tries, but Miles unlocked the phone and opened a text message to his friend in the Charlotte field office. This was far out of his jurisdiction, but I had seen before that any request from Miles got immediate attention from whoever received it. "Tell him hello... from me," Miles managed, closing his eyes again. He blew out long, steady breaths through parted lips.

I had just finished typing the text when Max appeared with the prescription bottle. "It says one before bedtime," she said nervously, handing the bottle over to me. "I don't know…"

I pushed send, shook out two pills, and handed them to Miles. I watched him wash down the pills with a gulp of water and then took the glass from his unsteady hand. I threaded my fingers through his again and leaned close. "Listen," I said softly. "I wanted to tell you this before, when you were hanging off the cliff, but I thought it might sound, you know, cheesy. Insincere." I smiled a little, locking onto his eyes, forcing everything else in the room, in the world, to fade away except, in that moment, the two of us. "I want you to know," I whispered, "that everything about my life changed for the better when you came into it. Everything. I wouldn't take back a minute of the time we've had together. Not the fights, not the laughter, not your stupid TV shows, not the way you win every board game, not even the way you make me crazy doing three things at once, not anything. I'm sorry I never said that before. Don't make me…" My eyes were wet and hot, and my voice grew thick. "Don't make me go on without you. Now that I know what it's like to be with you… just don't. Please."

He brought my hand to his bristled cheek. His grip was extraordinarily weak. The faintest of smiles curved his lips. "You're right," he murmured. "It was cheesy. And… I waited a long time to hear you say it."

I took several more breaths, smiling at him, fighting back tears. Then I got to my feet. "There's plenty of daylight," I said. "When I get to the bottom of the trail, I'll call emergency services and then drive your car back here on the service road. It shouldn't take more than a couple of hours. I need your keys."

"In my backpack," Miles said.

The front door opened on a blast of icy air, and I spun around, my heart in my throat. Cisco, who had been drying off in front of the woodstove, leapt to his feet. BJ almost dropped the mug of tea she was bringing to Miles, and Max stifled a scream. Reed's hand darted to the fireplace poker before we all recognized Parker, who held up an apologetic hand. I hadn't even realized he'd left the lodge.

"Sorry," he said, brushing melting ice crystals off his jacket. He came toward us. "Raine, you don't have to hike down. There's an ATV in that metal building, gassed up with keys in the ignition. We can be back in cell service range in fifteen, twenty minutes."

Relief washed through me. "Oh, thank God." I sorted out my jacket from the pile on the chair and pulled it on. Cisco, noticing, trotted to the door.

Parker said, "I'll go. You've done enough."

I zipped up my jacket. "Do you even know how to operate an ATV?"

He frowned a little. "How hard can it be?"

I pulled on my gloves. "I grew up on those things. And in weather like this, you need to know what you're doing."

He caught my arm and lowered his voice, half turning from the others. "There were two vehicles in the garage," he said. "I could see where the other one was parked and the tracks in the mud. Somebody got here before us and took the ATV out of here. He's probably still out there."

I thought about it, but not for long. If it was Theo, he would not still be hanging around. If it was the killer with the crossbow...

I looked quickly at Miles, whose face was taut with pain and whose eyes were closed. I looked back at Parker. "You've got the gun," I said, "and you're probably a better shot than I am. I'm a better ATV operator than you are. I go, you stay and keep these people safe. If I'm not back before dark, then"—I drew another deep breath— "make another plan."

I could see him struggling to find a more persuasive argument, but I did not give him a chance. I went quickly to Miles, checked the bandage on his leg, and leaned close to him. "Help is on the way," I said. "Hang in there. I'll be back before you know it."

"You... better be." His voice was heavy, and his words slurred a little. I hoped it was because of the Ambien, not blood loss and shock.

I smiled and squeezed his fingers. "I'm leaving you Cisco as a hostage."

I straightened and Reed said abruptly, "Hold on."

He left the room and returned in a moment with a red ski mask. "Don't know why I brought it," he said gruffly, looking embarrassed. "Know-it-all kid at the outfitter's store, when I said I was mountain camping... Anyway." He thrust the ski mask at me. "Here. This'll help keep the rain out of your face."

I smiled at the unexpected thoughtfulness as I took the mask. "Thanks, Reed."

Cisco was still waiting at the door, looking up at

me hopefully. I dropped to one knee to hug him. "Not this time, buddy," I said. My throat tightened with the words, remembering how I had regretted even bringing him along, and how many times he had proven his worth over the past twenty-four hours. Leaving him behind was almost as hard as leaving Miles. "Stay here and dry off, okay? I'll be back."

I kissed his silky muzzle and stood quickly, pulling on the ski mask. I left without another word, and the sound of Cisco's barking tore at my heart all the way across the yard.

CHAPTER THIRTY-FIVE

A smart man never left himself without options, and Jessup had several. The first was to cut his losses and move on, an idea that he had dismissed almost immediately. The second was to take out the whole group at the lodge with the AR-15 he had locked in the toolbox of the pickup truck, but the risk outweighed the gain there. One or more of them might be armed, and what would he have obtained even if he succeeded? Waste, that's what. No. He needed a live victim with a bank card and a passcode. That was the plan. It was important not to deviate from it.

There were two roads out of the lodge. The service road was longer and harder to access, and it was the one with which they were the least familiar. Frightened prey always took the fastest, most familiar route of escape, and they were very frightened now.

The hiking trail was the most direct route out, and, even though it was also the most dangerous in this weather, that was the one they would take.

Not all of them. Just one.

So he set his trap, and he moved off into the woods to wait. He burrowed deep into the shelter of a deadfall where he could watch the trail with his binoculars. He listened to the ping and click of ice falling in the woods, to the rush of wind in the naked branches overhead, and the sounds were music to him. The woods were his home. The smell of cold earth, the dark shadows and swells, the rustles and sighs and groans and squeals of lives lived and lives extinguished that were woven by the centuries into the very fabric of this forest... they were part of him. He owned them all. He was not cold. He was not tired. The icy shards that drifted from the sky today were no strangers to him, no impediment to his goals. They were, in fact, his friend. Because they were, at this moment, his prey's worst enemy. All he had to do was exercise the hunter's greatest virtue: patience.

When he heard the distant sound of an ATV engine, he couldn't help smiling. Plan, persistence, patience. You couldn't lose.

He watched through his binoculars as the rider plowed down the road, skidding from one side to the other over the ice patches, accelerating beyond the point of control, cornering on two wheels. Inevitably, the vehicle plowed into the barricade Jessup had dragged across the trail, went airborne, and landed on its side. The rider was thrown clear a half-dozen feet down the trail.

Jessup didn't even rush getting to the scene of the accident. That fool wasn't going anywhere.

When he reached the site, he thought his victim might be dead, and he felt a brief, infuriating surge of annoyance. But no. Luck was on his side this time. Bleeding from a head wound, unconscious, but there was a pulse. Jessup noted the weirdly twisted arm with regret; he would have enjoyed breaking it, bone by bone, himself. He went through the pockets and found a wallet containing a couple of hundred dollars and, yes, bank cards. He pocketed the cards and cash and tossed the wallet aside. He quickly bound the hands and feet and dragged his victim off the trail into the woods. It wasn't that much farther to the truck and Jessup could carry the rider if he had to, but he hoped he didn't have to. He could spare a few minutes to wait until the prey came to and could walk unassisted. Patience was the key. Jessup settled down to wait.

That was when the unexpected happened.

CHAPTER THIRTY-SIX

The trail was slick with mud and ice, and after the second time I almost rolled the vehicle I thought, Parker never would have made it this far. The tracks of a four-wheeler that had gone before me complicated matters, threatening to bog down my tires or throw me off balance every time I hit them. I didn't allow myself to think about who had gone before. All that mattered was that they were in front of me, not behind. Not lying in wait somewhere near the lodge. Not siting Miles or BJ or Reed or Max or Parker through a crossbow.

I learned to keep the ATV toward the side of the trail and avoid the ruts created by my predecessor, and all I had to worry about was avoiding trees and ice slicks. The creek, the part I was worried about, proved to be no problem at all. The tires spun once or twice, soaking my pants and boots with icy water, but for the most part, I sailed right through.

The roar of the engine and the rhythm of the wheels were hypnotic, and I settled into a kind of alternate state, guiding the vehicle by instinct while my thoughts raced along an entirely different plane. I should have told them to remove Miles's boot before the swelling cut off circulation. I should have told BJ to pack the wound in tea bags to slow down the bleeding and to force fluids to prevent shock. I should have reminded them to keep his leg elevated and pack it in ice to reduce the swelling.

Clearly, I had taken too many emergency first aid courses. And clearly, they had not been enough when it counted.

I was the one who had untied Theo's hands. I was the one who had let him push Miles over the cliff. It was my fault. And I was the only one who could make it right.

The landscape of the mind is as dark and as treacherous as the depths of any ancient forest. Vicious predators lurk in the shadows, waiting to tear out your heart and strip your will of the instinct to survive. Killer truths lurk in the shadows, daring you to confront them. Every careless word I had ever spoken, every bad decision I had ever made, every time I had ever stared happiness in the face and turned away... those are the things that battered me like the ice pellets that pelted my mask as I sped down the trail. The things I should have done, the things I had failed to do, the things I might never get a chance to do because the person I wanted to do them with was now in jeopardy of his life in the middle of nowhere, without me. Because of me.

Survival begins in the mind.

So absorbed was I in the jungle of my own dark thoughts that I almost didn't see the obstacle on the trail until I was upon it. The ice was coming down in sheets with the velocity of the ATV, caking on my ski mask and stabbing at my eyes, and I had to squint to see through it. A pile of fallen debris lay across the trail not twenty feet ahead. Before it was a river of rutted tire tracks and beyond it a tangle of metal I couldn't quite define. I slammed on the brakes and the ATV went into a skid, spinning in a full circle before I regained my senses and eased up on the brake, tweaking the accelerator, bringing the vehicle to a hard stop with its nose in the ditch and the handlebars in my rib cage less than a foot before the collision with the deadfall.

I sat there for a moment, the breath knocked out of me, gasping like a beached fish and holding my bruised ribs. When the world righted itself and I could once again suck cold air into my lungs, I pushed away from the machine and slowly climbed off. The obstacle in front of me wasn't high, but it was more than the ATV could safely climb. And what was that on the other side? Damn it. I couldn't afford to waste time with this.

Still rubbing my aching ribs with one hand, I climbed over the thicket of fallen saplings and tree branches. A match for the ATV I was riding lay on its side a few feet from the fallen trees, deep skid marks plotting its progress. Apparently, the rider had tried to jump the obstacle, or had been going too fast to stop and had gone airborne. This was the result. And the rider was nowhere to be found.

Ice was starting to cake around the eyeholes of the ski mask, weighing down my lashes and obscuring my vision. I pulled the mask off and stuffed it in my pocket, then pulled my hood back up over my head. I saw blood on the ground a few feet away from the wreck, partially obscured by crystals of ice. And I saw drag marks in the mud, leading toward the woods at the side of the trail. I stood staring at them, dread congealing in the pit of my stomach.

I never heard him coming. Not the snap of a twig, the rustle of a leaf, the slide of a footstep. Suddenly there was an arm around my neck, hard and harsh, pulling me back against a sinewy form that smelled of blood and sweat and smoke and dead things. Instinctively I clawed at the grip, my feet sliding on the ice, my throat closing as he pressed harder. I felt the tip of something cold and sharp and metal just behind my ear.

He said, low and close, "I hoped it would be you." He paused. "Where's your dog?"

"Not... here." My voice was hoarse and squeaky, choked by the force of his forearm against my trachea. But as soon as I spoke, he eased the pressure a little. I could breathe.

"Shame," he said. "I like dogs."

My head was tilted backward in his grip and there was just enough latitude for me to roll my eyes upward and look at him. It was the man with the ginger beard from the camp last night. The one who had stolen the ranger's uniform. The ranger he had killed and dismembered. He wasn't wearing the uniform now, though. My fingers were gripping an arm wrapped in weatherproof camo. The point of a knife dug into the flesh just below my ear. And like a movie unreeling at super-fast speed, I saw what was going to happen next. He would drag me off into the woods and rape and torture me because that was what he did and there was no one to stop him. He was stronger than I was, and he had done this before. He would not make a mistake; I would not escape. When he was tired of me, he would kill me, or I would die of my wounds. He would dismember my body and scatter the pieces for the carrion eaters, and no one would ever know what happened to me. Not Miles, not the others at the lodge who were waiting for me to bring help, not my aunt and uncle or Casey or Melanie or my friends back home. They would spend their shattered lives alternating between grief and shock and false hope and nothing would ever be the same for them.

Except that was not what was going to happen. I wouldn't let it. People were depending on me, and I would not die at the hands of this man.

Deliberately, almost as if to demonstrate gratitude for the lessening of the pressure on my throat, I loosened my fingers. Showing no resistance. Showing trust.

"The other ATV," I managed. "What happened to

the rider?"

"Oh, don't you worry," said the man, "he's just fine. And you and me and him, we're going to have ourselves a high time. Yes, indeed." He jammed his knee into the back of my thigh. "Now move, and don't give me any trouble."

He dragged me forward a step and I pretended to lose my balance, struggling not to fall. "You're too smart for this," I said. "You know you are." He stopped, momentarily intrigued by my words. "These woods are going to be swarming with law enforcement before dark. A park ranger is dead. Do you think her colleagues aren't looking for her?" I knew the ranger had planned vacation time, but he didn't. "They'll find the bodies. Everyone at the lodge can give a description of you. It's time to cut your losses. There's nowhere to hide."

He dragged me forward again, down the trail. "You've got one hostage already, right?" I went on, gasping for breath as his arm tightened on my throat. "Another one just complicates things. Slows you down. You've been watching us. You know I'm not stupid. I'll escape if I can and even if I can't, the trying will only make your life harder."

He said, "You make some good points. But I think you underestimate me. I have a certain amount of experience in these matters. I know what I'm doing."

"Death row is full of people who knew what they were doing," I said. My voice hoarsened as his arm tightened. My chest ached with the effort to draw a breath. "Let me go. Leave Theo behind. You'll have a solid start. You're savvy enough to disappear if you have enough time. This is your chance. Take it."

He hesitated, and for a moment I thought I might have actually gotten through to him. Then he said, "Shut up and move."

He pushed me hard, and I took a stumbling step forward. His arm tightened on my throat when I almost fell. A strangled cry escaped my lips. And out of the corner of my eye, I saw a figure step out of the shadows on the opposite side of the trail. A cold voice said, "Take your goddamn hands off my sister."

It was Casey, and he had a gun.

CHAPTER THIRTY-SEVEN

It was him. It was Casey, his curly blond hair pulled back in a ponytail and frizzing on top, his denim jacket splotched with icy rainwater, his face set into hard, ferocious lines as he leveled a Ruger at the man who held me hostage.

I gasped, "Casey!" but even as I did the man swung around with a short but vicious change of position, one arm locked against my throat and the full blade of the knife in the other hand pressed beneath my jawline. I stretched my head back, trying to avoid the sting of the blade, and once again clawed at the arm that cut off my breath.

The man's breath hissed in my ear. "Well now," he said, "we have ourselves an interesting situation here."

Casey's hands tightened on the grip of the gun, and he shifted his weight, balancing himself for the shot.

He did not take his eyes off the other man. He said lowly, "Let her go."

My captor seemed remarkably calm and unruffled, though his arm against my neck was like corded steel. The blade beneath my jaw seemed to dig deeper every time I breathed so I tried to breathe shallowly.

"I'm not going to do that," replied the other man pleasantly. "So you've got a decision to make, don't you? Now, looking at you, I can tell you're a pretty good shot. Probably not the first time you've faced another man across the barrel of a gun. Not afraid to do what has to be done when it gets right down to it. How'm I doing? Pretty good, right? Studying people is what you might call a hobby of mine."

"Put down the knife," Casey said, his aim unwavering, "and let her go."

"You're thinking right now you could make the headshot," the man went on, "and from this distance, you probably could. But here's my question for you. Can you shoot me before I cut her throat?"

I pushed my head back as far as I could, gasping for breath. "He's...killed three... people!" I croaked. "Casey!"

I felt something warm and wet trickle down the front of my neck. Casey's eyes for the first time left the man long enough to flicker to my throat, then quickly back again. The man repeated, "Can you?"

That time I felt the bite of the blade and I cried out. I couldn't help it.

Casey slowly put the gun on the ground and straightened up again, hands at shoulder height.

My captor moved the blade away from my skin. "I admire a man who makes good decisions," he said. "Now, kick the gun over here."

I begged Casey with my eyes, but I didn't know what I was begging him to do. *Don't let this man kill someone else. Don't take any chances. Don't …*

There was a sudden crashing in the woods behind us, a great rushing of movement. Instinctively, we all turned toward it and the killer, twisting around, was forced to release his grip on me just enough for me to swing my foot back and kick him hard in the knee. The half-second of surprise was enough for me to wrest my way away from him just as Cisco scrambled over the barricade in the road and ran toward me. Cisco, my beautiful, incorrigible, soaking wet golden retriever with a mind of his own and a refusal to take no for an answer. I lunged for him, and Casey dived to the ground, grabbing the gun. I caught Cisco around the neck and, slipping in the icy mud, dragged him to the ground with me just as a gunshot split the air, then another. I wound my fingers around Cisco's collar and crawled to the weeds at the side of the trail, dragging Cisco with me, as another shot cracked.

All of this took place in less than five seconds, the time it takes a semiautomatic to fire three successive shots, but every detail is exquisitely clear in my memory. Cisco's heavy panting breath in my ear, his cold wet coat beneath my cheek, the gagging, coughing sounds of my own breath as I dragged it in through bruised vocal cords. Ice clicking on the ground and the smell of cordite.

Then Casey's hand on my arm, pulling me to my feet. His voice, ragged and harsh. "Jesus, girl, are you okay? I think I winged him. Come on, we've got to get out of here." Then, "Cisco, my man, where the hell did you come from?"

I tried to stand but my knees wouldn't support me. I clung to Cisco, gasping and sobbing. He was trembling with excitement and exertion. So was I. Casey knelt beside me, his arm around my shoulders. "How bad are you hurt? You're bleeding. Can you walk? We really, really need to book, kiddo. That guy might be coming back, and I don't want to be here when he does."

Finally, I was able to lift my head, to look around. The man with the beard was gone. I didn't know how far. I clutched Casey's arm. "How did you … where did you… What are you doing here?"

"Your watch," he said. He tried again to pull me to my feet and this time was more successful. "I got an emergency message from it. I might've thought it was a mistake, but I got one from Miles at the same time. You okay? Can you make it?"

I stared at him. "Miles? Messaged you?"

"His watch did. He must've programmed in my number as his emergency contact."

And even in that crazed, desperate moment, it struck me. Miles had called on Casey. He did trust him, after all. He trusted him, as it turned out, with his life.

Casey urged me forward down the trail. Cisco trotted beside me, still panting hard, his eyes upturned on my every move and looking absurdly, ridiculously happy just to be here.

"I called the park service and told them to check on you," Casey rushed on, "but figured it wouldn't hurt to start up this way in the meantime." His voice was choppy and uneven, and he slipped on the ice as he hurried me along. "I got a call from them halfway up saying the lodge was empty and they couldn't devote any more resources to a search without proof something was wrong. What in the *hell* is going on, if you don't mind my asking?"

"We've got to… got to get cell service." My throat burned with every word, but I couldn't get them out fast enough. "Miles is hurt. Need a hospital. That man… three people dead. He has a crossbow. Theo… I don't know what happened to him. We have to… have to get help."

"Almost there," Casey said, pulling me forward. "My truck is just around the corner."

Almost there. I hadn't realized how far I had come. While I was being held at knifepoint by a bloodthirsty killer I was literally within steps of safety. As though to illustrate the point, there was a sudden buzzing and chiming from my coat pocket. I stumbled to a stop and unzipped my pocket, fumbling for the phones. My phone was lit up with an incoming call, and so was Miles's. At some point I must have passed through a reception zone long enough for my texts to go through because the caller ID on my phone said, "911 Dispatch."

I thrust Miles's phone at Casey and answered my own. "This is the 911 operator," the voice on the other end said. "We had…"

"Yes!" I gasped. "Yes, this is an emergency! We need an ambulance…"

I heard Casey saying into Miles's phone, "No, this is not Young. This must be his phone. Who the hell is this?"

Casey pulled me along, forcing me into a run. Cisco saw the vehicles parked up ahead and galloped toward them. Miles's car, Casey's pickup, and an older, dirty brown truck I didn't recognize.

"…and police," I said, breathing hard as I tried to keep up with Casey. "We're at Hidden Lodge near the Great Smoky Mountains Park. There's a man…"

"…Real shitstorm here," Casey was saying, his voice punctuated with his jogging steps. "We've got injuries, at least three dead, some lunatic with a knife…"

"Hurry," I cried, my voice breaking with desperation. "Just please hurry!"

The lights on Casey's truck flashed and the locks beeped open. He threw open the passenger door and Cisco bounded inside. Casey pushed me in after him and ran around to the driver's side.

"Ma'am," the dispatcher said calmly in my ear, "just stay on the line." Casey climbed into the driver's seat and started the engine. And then she said the sweetest words I have ever heard. "Help is on the way."

CHAPTER THIRTY-EIGHT

Forty-eight hours later, Casey, Parker, Cisco, and I were in a private family waiting room just outside the hospital chapel in Knoxville, Tennessee. Parker, like Miles, knows how to throw his weight around when necessary, and we had been granted every allowable convenience, from private showers to outside catering. On the other hand, with all the police going back and forth to interview us and reporters trying to get to us, keeping us isolated in a quiet part of the hospital probably worked out better for the staff, too.

Casey and Parker had gotten rooms in a nearby hotel, and I think a room was reserved for me as well. But I had spent the previous nights on one of those uncomfortable chairs in Miles's room, sleeping in snatches in between nurses' visits. He was going to be fine, they told me. A couple of months in a cast and no one would ever know what had happened. Except we would never forget it.

In the times when he was awake and not being tortured by the nurses, we snuggled and talked about things. I asked him why he had changed his emergency contact number to Casey's, which was, if you thought about it, the one thing that had saved all our lives. He said, "Baby, Casey is a scoundrel and a card cheat, we all know that…"

"He is not a card cheat," I objected immediately, bristling.

"But," Miles went on, "he's got one important trait in common with you. There is absolutely nothing he wouldn't do for family. And, like it or not, I guess we're his family now. So, taking all things into consideration and given that he was the most geographically accessible person under the circumstances, I changed my emergency number."

"Totally logical," I agreed.

"Absolutely."

"But Casey is not a card cheat."

Miles wisely did not reply.

Miles talked about selling off the majority of his business and concentrating on local residential building projects, which had always been his first love. No more overseas travel, no more exotic acquisitions, no more organizing rescues for employees who were being held hostage by terrorists. He had talked about this before, particularly since he'd become Melanie's sole guardian. But this time, I thought he might actually do it.

I kept him up to date on the investigation, because he would have been impatient with me if I had not. But we didn't talk about it beyond the bare facts. Neither of us wanted to revisit that time in our heads again.

Miles's mother had wanted to drive up immediately, of course, but Miles and I had discussed it before they took him to surgery, and he'd instructed me that under no circumstances was Melanie to be taken out of school and driven to another state because her father was in the hospital. He was absolutely right, and I was able to convince his mother of that without too much trouble. The child had lost her mother not that long ago, and we all knew Melanie and her imagination. She would have concocted an entire apocalyptic scenario before they even reached Tennessee. Miles had FaceTimed her this morning before she went to school, made light of the broken leg, and told her we'd all be home in time to taste the flatbread her class was baking on a rock. She had seemed much less interested in the broken leg than in the fact that Cisco was allowed in the hospital. Miles and I considered that a job well done.

An aide knocked on the half-open door of the waiting room and brought in an enormous arrangement of tiger lilies, reporting, "I thought you'd like to have these here. Mr. Young's room is filling up."

Miles's room was only a few doors down, and there were already far too many arrangements there —roses from Aunt Mart, hydrangeas from Miles's mother and Melanie, and a massive arrangement of every flower under the sun from his office. This was not to even mention the assortment of balloons and potted plants, most of them from business acquaintances I'd never heard of. The more colorful flower arrangements had been moved to the chapel; the others would be distributed to other patients once Miles was discharged.

The aide placed the flowers on a console table and bent to greet Cisco as he came wagging up. "Hi, there, pretty boy. You doing okay? Got everything you need? You know I came up here just to see you, don't you?"

Cisco, a registered therapy dog who carried his credentials in his backpack, was qualified to go into any hospital, nursing home, school, or other public facility in the country. The hospital could have refused him entry, of course, but I don't think anyone, looking at me when I rushed into the emergency room with Miles, blood-stained and wild-eyed, dared try. At one point someone—Parker? Casey? The hospital family liaison? —even had dog bowls and a package of gourmet dog food delivered. With all the stress and commotion that our arrival had brought to the hospital, Cisco continued to do his therapy work for both the staff and the police interviewers.

According to Parker, Cisco escaped the lodge minutes after I left, when Reed opened the door to bring in more firewood. Cutting through the woods to pick up my trail, Cisco actually had less distance to travel than I had. And while Reed had been insisting that he be allowed to go after Cisco and while Parker had been insisting that the doors remain barricaded,

Cisco had been well on his way to saving my life.

Cisco, with wagging tail and happy grin, assured the young aide that he was, in fact, doing just fine, and I read the card attached to the flowers. "No more wild adventures," it said. I smiled as I told Parker, "From BJ."

He held up his phone. "She must've sent them from the plane. I just got a text saying she's home safely. And she's taking two weeks off."

I replied, "Only two weeks?"

Everyone but Parker had taken the first flight home as soon as the police released them to do so. Parker, the senior man on site, had stayed behind to deal with all the complications pursuant to the tragic retreat, and there were a lot of them: Theo's betrayal, the head of the company out of commission, the course instructor murdered. I couldn't tell the private security men from the FBI agents as they came and went, but Parker handled it all.

Theo had been found bound, gagged, and semiconscious, locked in the brown pickup truck at the trailhead. He was now being treated for a concussion and broken arm at a smaller hospital across town. I was not privy to what he had told the police, and I didn't much care. Parker said he'd be charged with corporate espionage, but since he hadn't actually stolen anything of value, a good lawyer would probably get him off. The chances of him ever working in tech again, though—or in any corporate capacity—were slim. Again, I didn't care.

A massive manhunt was underway for my assailant, the killer of Rick Steele, Ian Wharton, and the park ranger, Meg Oakley. So far, nothing. But, they kept telling us, it had only been forty-eight hours. Fugitives had been captured under similar circumstances after weeks, even months of searching. In the case of Eric Rudolph, it had taken years. I did not find that at all reassuring.

Casey, who couldn't resist flirting with every pretty girl who came in—and there had been a lot of them—took a piece of roast beef from one of the deli trays on the buffet table and said, "He'll do tricks for roast beef. Watch this."

He took Cisco through one of his dance moves—twirling on his back legs—and the aide laughed with delight. I was about to tell Casey to knock it off with the treats but just then Detective Sarah Hunnicut came in. Casey was as easily distracted as Cisco in the presence of another attractive young woman, and the aide quickly excused herself and left.

There were so many law enforcement agencies involved I couldn't keep track of them all, but this detective, who had been one of the first on the scene and who I thought was with the police from the town nearest the lodge, had been the most helpful.

She greeted Cisco, refused the cup of coffee Casey offered her, and turned to me. "I finished interviewing your fiancé," she said. "I think we've got all we need for now. I hear you're planning to leave tomorrow."

I nodded. Miles was cleared to travel home by private ambulance, where his recovery would be supervised by home healthcare nurses and, if necessary, specialists from Asheville and Atlanta. He would be much, much better off there. All we wanted, any of us, was to put this place behind us.

I said, "You've got our contact information. None of us is hard to find."

"Well, it looks like the FBI will be taking the lead on this case anyway," she replied. "There've been some reports that might link the perp to similar crimes in other states. I just wanted to bring you up to date on what we have so far." She took a notebook from the pocket of her corduroy jacket and consulted it. "Fingerprints on the truck and other items trace back to one Patrick Henry Jessup, 63. Arrested in Utah for shoplifting, served ten days, and kidnapping in Georgia, released for lack of evidence. We found a hatchet and a hacksaw in the toolbox of his truck with traces of blood on them. Results aren't in yet, but it's fresh enough to match that of the dismembered victim we found in the woods. Also several automatic weapons and… well, I guess you don't need to know the details." She looked a little apologetic as she flipped the notebook closed.

I took a shaky breath and Casey put a sympathetic hand on my back. "That is one sick dude," he said. "Any sign?"

"Don't worry," she replied confidently, "We've got every law enforcement officer from here to the North Carolina border on this, and now that the weather's lifted, dogs and drones and helicopters scouring the woods. We'll get him."

I said, because I just couldn't not say it, "That park is over five hundred thousand acres. He's a professional."

She held my gaze and repeated, "He's wounded, he's cut off from his supplies, he's on foot and desperate. We'll get him."

I wished I could believe her.

The door opened again, and Miles was there, a nurse pushing his wheelchair, his casted leg extended before him. He was in a hospital gown and robe, and to be honest, looked exactly like a man who had almost died and had major surgery thirty-two hours before. But he had a chrysanthemum pinned to the front of his hospital robe and when I saw it, I burst into delighted laughter. He was Miles, the man I loved, and the memories of the past two days, the dread of a remorseless killer hiding in the shadows only a few dozen miles away, all faded into the simple joy of the moment. He was here. I was here. We were alive.

"Hey," he said, winking, "we have an appointment. Let's not keep the man waiting."

I said, "Right with you."

"Step on it," he advised as the nurse wheeled him away. "Nurse Ratched here said I could only be out of bed for fifteen minutes."

I turned to the detective and apologized, "Sorry. This is important."

The way she smiled back told me she understood. "I'll be in touch," she promised.

When she was gone, Parker smiled at me and said, "Are you ready for this?"

Impulsively I hugged his neck. "Thank you for staying," I said.

I turned to Casey and hugged him hard. "Thank you for coming to save me." The events of the past few days had taught me it was important to say things like that.

"Hey, no problem," he allowed.

I looked at both men, beaming. "Okay," I said. "Let's do this."

I started for the door, but Casey said, "Hey, hold on."

He thrust a bouquet of tiger lilies, torn from BJ's arrangement and still dripping water, into my hand. "Now," he said, "we're ready."

And that was how, in the chapel of a hospital in Tennessee, I came to marry the man who knew me well enough to play me on Broadway, the man who loved me enough to start a fight with me, the man who never failed to remind me I was enough; my hero, my legend, the love of my life. Because if this survival retreat had taught me nothing else, it was that some things should never be put off.

Casey and Cisco walked me down the aisle. Parker was the best man. The bride wore clean sweatpants and a Great Smoky Mountains National Park sweatshirt and carried a bouquet of randomly wilting tiger lilies. The groom wore a leg cast and a ridiculous chrysanthemum pinned to his hospital robe. Everyone smelled like wet dog and campfire smoke. It was my dream wedding.

Of course, Miles's mother and my aunt Mart would be devastated to know they'd missed the wedding, not to mention the tantrum Melanie would pitch, so we'll have another ceremony this spring with fancy dresses and champagne and a full-on band with dancing into the night. Parker said he'd come, and we'll invite BJ and Max and Reed and pretend like it's all for the first time. Meantime, we're keeping our marriage a secret, just for us.

So don't tell anyone.

As for Patrick Henry Jessup... yeah, they didn't catch him. Sometimes I wake in the middle of the night, shaking and gasping, remembering the ice, the cold, the blood. Miles will hold me and soothe me and tell me everything is okay, and I believe him, for the moment, because he was there, and he understands.

But there are things he doesn't understand, things he doesn't know. There are things I can't even entirely explain, but when I was held prisoner by Jessup, when his arm was across my throat and his whisper was in my ear, I understood this: there are master predators in this world. There are those to whom killing is a pastime and survival is a credo. They are smarter than us, more determined than us, and they have nothing to lose. They are virtually undefeatable.

Jessup is just such a man, and he is out there, somewhere, waiting to strike again.

I just hope we're ready when he does.

The Saga of the Hunter continues with UNDEFEATABLE: A Buck Lawson Mystery

Blood River Mystery #3

Coming in 2025

ABOUT THE AUTHOR

Donna Ball

Donna Ball is the author of over 100 books under a variety of pseudonyms. Though she has been published in virtually every genre, she is best known for her work in women's fiction, mystery and suspense. Her novels have been translated into multiple languages and published around the world. Her most popular series are the award-winning Raine Stockton Dog Mystery series, the Dogleg Island Mystery series, The Blood River Mystery series, and the Ladybug Farm series. All are available now in paperback in bookstores everywhere, as audiobook downloads, and in digital format for your e-reader.

Donna lives in the heart of the Blue Ridge Divide in a restored Victorian barn which was the inspiration for the bestselling A YEAR ON LADYBUG FARM. She spends her spare time hiking, painting, and enjoying canine sports with her three dogs.

MORE BY DONNA BALL

The Raine Stockton Dog Mystery Series

Books in Order

SMOKY MOUNTAIN TRACKS

RAPID FIRE

GUN SHY

BONE YARD

SILENT NIGHT

THE DEAD SEASON

ALL THAT GLITTERS: A Holiday Short Story e book

HIGH IN TRIAL

DOUBLE DOG DARE

HOME OF THE BRAVE

DOG DAYS

LAND OF THE FREE

DEADFALL

THE DEVIL'S DEAL

MURDER CREEK

ANGELS IN THE SNOW: A Raine Stockton Short Novella (Also available in DECK THE HALLS: A HOLIDAY MYSTERY ANTHOLOGY)

THE JUDGES DAUGHTER

DEAD MAN'S TRAIL

* * *

The Blood River Mystery Series

UNFIXABLE: A Buck Lawson Mystery

WELCOME TO BETHLEHEM: A Buck Lawson Short Novella (

Also available in DECK THE HALLS: A HOLIDAY MYSTERY ANTHOLOGY)

UNSTOPPABLE A Buck Lawson Mystery

❃ ❃ ❃

Spine-chilling suspense by Donna Ball

SHATTERED

NIGHT FLIGHT

SANCTUARY

EXPOSURE

❃ ❃ ❃

Also by Donna Ball

The Ladybug Farm Series

For every woman who ever had a dream... or a friend

A Year on Ladybug Farm
At Home on Ladybug Farm
Love Letters from Ladybug Farm

Christmas on Ladybug Farm
Recipes from Ladybug Farm
Vintage Ladybug Farm

A Wedding on Ladybug Farm

The Hummingbird House
Christmas at the Hummingbird House
The Hummingbird House Presents

www.ingramcontent.com/pod-product-compliance
Lightning Source LLC
Chambersburg PA
CBHW060521160726
47991CB00001B/133